A Western Analects

Marvin Bram

Library of Congress Number#:		00-192644
ISBN #:	Hardcover	0-7388-3982-5
	Softcover	0-7388-3069-0

This book was printed in the United States of America.

To order additional copies of this book, contact:
Xlibris Corporation
1-888-7-XLIBRIS
www.Xlibris.com
Orders@Xlibris.com

Contents

Part I

PART I

The Teacher

1.

Death

"Welcome, welcome. Look at you. Wonderful."

The teacher ushered his four friends in and nodded toward the large, comfortable kitchen. Bent forward with age, he slowly made his way behind them through the music room to the familiar round kitchen table. There was not much more to the house. (The teacher slept in the music room.) A chaotic vegetable garden and citrus orchard surrounded the house, and a pine and maple woods undisturbed except for a dirt road surrounded the garden.

"Please sit. My grand-daughter made the torte. You'll love it. I'll put on coffee."

One of the guests, William, had been a colleague of the teacher. The three others had been his students, the oldest, Eleanor, forty years before. They gathered at the remote house for a day every spring.

Eleanor, normally calm, seemed agitated. She had retired from a city hospital in the midwest earlier in the year.

"I think I'll move nearer here," she said on taking a place at the table. "I've had enough of cities. Enough of nursing, of sickness."

The teacher sat next to Eleanor. He took her hand.

"You've relieved so much suffering, Eleanor. You should be proud."

"Maybe the trouble isn't what I said. Retirement is my last transition before the truly last one; maybe it's that the next big event is my death. I was planning to be giddy with happiness to be de-institutionalized at last, but before I turned around, death began to work on me. It's ridiculous. I should be used to death, having seen so much of it at the hospital."

Jerry was twenty-six. "You're not alone, Eleanor. I'm supposed to be young enough to still feel immortal. That's a laugh. I passed the bar a couple of weeks ago—the transition I'm in, starting what you're finishing—and I alternately feel ready to live and afraid to die."

A long two minutes of silence fell on the table. Jerry resumed.

"Last year we skipped the subject because of the Chinese material. The Confucians didn't take it up, so we didn't. Did we know so much about living that we could talk about dying, they said, right? Frustrating."

"Isn't it time?" Eleanor asked the teacher.

He gently let loose her hand and slumped back in his chair, his eyes half closed.

"It's time."

Catherine, somewhat older than Jerry and an artist in wood and stone, had been arranging to move her parents in with her. She worried about three generations in the same house. Her father wasn't expected to live much longer. How would her children take his death?

"My father is dying," she said softly, abstractedly.

"That's where we have to begin," the teacher said, turning toward Catherine, "with the death of loved ones, not with our own death. You must give yourself to the great project of becoming your father, Catherine—not merely living with your father, or even taking care of him, but becoming him, remaining yourself and adding him to yourself. That is the key to his dying without the worst worry a parent can have. It's also the key to your being alright, and more than alright, after he dies. Perhaps Confucius missed an opportunity. Perhaps if you know about death, you know about life."

"My becoming him spares him his worst worry?" Catherine said.

"A loving father, about to die, sees upcoming loss in the eyes of his child. He fears she'll feel diminished after he dies. He doesn't want you to live like that, reduced. The thought of it, and his helplessness to do anything about it, pain him. So you do something our distant ancestors probably did. You show your father that you're adding him to yourself. You make it clear. After his death, after the shock of it, you won't be less than you were because he's gone, but more. By an ancient act of mind, you will have dissolved the boundary between the two of you, and you will have become him-plus-you. It's when he understands this that he can die in peace, and it's when you understand it that you can be with him in the best way now, and live an enlarged life later, afterward."

Jerry looked concerned. "The weakening of that boundary sounds—what—pathological, like some kind of schizophrenia."

The teacher smiled. "It *is* a pathology, if you're replaced by the other person, one for one, and if you have no control of your boundary condition. Catherine's task is to add a person to herself, not to replace one person by another, and the project will be completely under her control. You might say that what happens is a willed strengthening of the imagination in the interests of those you love and in the name of your own growth. Adding to yourself this way continues as you get older, with the deaths of the people you've loved. So it's good to be old, something not many people believe."

"That growth happens at the deaths of a person's loved ones seems unusual, doesn't it?" Jerry asked.

"Isn't the alternative terrible?" the teacher replied. "Continuous loss. Dying empty yourself because those you've loved have died and there has been no augmentation. What good is consciousness if it's passive and it shrinks with time? That can't be what it's for."

William spoke slowly but excitedly. "It must have been that way in the totemic world. I remember how my friends would debate totemism, the real mystery of the human condition, they claimed. But what if a person were, as you put it, boundary-dissolved," William looked at the teacher, pursing his lips, his eyes shining, "boundary-dissolved for an animal, the totem animal, and for every human member of his clan, *and* for a representation of the animal, the totem, and even for the origin-story of the clan, for the words themselves. Then, you see, an injury to the animal would injure the clan; the story mis-told would injure the clan. Taking care of any *one* element would take care of the whole—the persons, animals, amulets, words. Ha! There's responsibility for you."

The teacher laughed. "Look at marrying inside the clan, which you weren't supposed to do. How could you do it? The other clanspeople were boundary-dissolved with respect to you; you'd be marrying yourself. You had to marry outside the clan just to be marrying somebody *else*."

"There you have a world that both made distinctions and un-made them," William mused. "The other clans had, I mean were, other animals, other stories. Distinctions. And in my clan, we're all of us each other. The absence of distinctions. You can't help wondering whether a mode of life that does both, make and un-make distinctions, that puts up boundaries and takes them down, works better than our own, just on the guess that full use of the mind is a better thing than partial use. It's obvious that our own culture is committed to distinction-making exclusively. But human beings probably lived in one kind of totemic order or another over most of the planet for most of the time we've been human."

"We only began to de-value boundary-dissolution with the rise of cities," the teacher said. "We can have it back."

"I often feel that my children are me," Catherine said. "When you love someone the distinction begins to go."

"Exactly," the teacher said.

Jerry asked the teacher if he lived in some sort of totemic world here in the woods.

"I try to be—the verb 'to be' taken pretty far—all the people I've ever loved and who aren't alive. I, we, are a council, perhaps like a council twenty thousand years ago in William's world, but in my imagination. We talk, tell stories, tell each other jokes, all the time."

"You know that each of us will become you some day, a long way off I hope," Eleanor said.

"Do we get the whole council?" Jerry cracked.

Catherine glared at Jerry.

The teacher laughed again, "You get the whole bunch of us. We're moving in."

2.

Kindness

"You said we could have boundary-dissolution back," William said.

The teacher cut the torte into five big pieces. "It should be moved into the social order as kindness," he said while distributing the heavily laden plates, "the kindness based on becoming the other person. Then the same mental activity that consoles a dying parent or anyone else we love and who loves us, and that holds out the possibility of real growth following the deaths of the people we love—that same activity informs everyday life, our ordinary interactions. Kindness becomes the prime virtue."

Jerry poured the coffee. "That's a lot to say. It leaves intelligence out, it seems to me. William remembers polite discussions in faculty clubs; I remember bitter arguments among us kids in the lousy neighborhood we grew up in. 'Is it better to be smart or nice, smart or nice?' 'Smart,' I said, 'obviously.' I'd get out of there by being smart. And I did."

"You were right?" the teacher asked.

"I got into a national law school. I'll wear English suits and drive a Mercedes. I don't know if I was right. How do *I* know? One of us, the nicest kid among us, kind absolutely by your definition, quit school when he was fifteen. He said he wasn't smart enough or good looking enough—that killed me, even then—to be OK in America. He went to Mexico. We couldn't believe it. I heard from him a few months ago. He married a woman who he says he doesn't deserve. They have a store. He sews up torn clothes, repairs shoes, fixes busted toys. They sound happy."

"Do you have to choose between intelligence and kindness?" Eleanor asked.

"There's short answer and a long answer," the teacher began. "The short answer is, Yes, you have to choose. I know that this surprises you, because we're supposed to have everything we want in an unproblematical way. But there are problems. Century after century of choosing intelligence has compressed our society into a half-society; and often enough the claim was that both kindness and intelligence *were* being chosen. Sometimes the claim was made in good faith, sometimes in bad faith; the result was the same—a half-society. We must choose kindness, period." The teacher paused, then resumed. "There's an unexpected benefit to choosing kindness over intelligence. In a wonderful way, you get both. Kindness actually possesses an intelligence of its own, unique to it. Intelligence, on the other hand, has no kindness of its own."

Catherine became more and more animated as the teacher spoke. "I can't tell you how glad I am to hear you say that. All my life in school, intelligence was everything. I felt like Jerry's friend. And it was always measured by how quick you were to make a distinction, or see a distinction somewhere that somebody else didn't see. Did I use the right word in that sentence when I was called on in third grade? No no; I didn't distinguish between the *almost* right word I used and the *precisely* right word I was supposed to have used. Result, I was humiliated before the other kids. Did I distinguish between this book and that, better book in high school? No no; I liked them both. Wrong. How about these two paintings by El Greco in college? Same thing, over and over again. This is different from that. That is better than this. It made me sadder every year. I'd been a happy kid, too."

Eleanor joined in. "When I was young, I liked every violin performance I heard on the radio and on records. Then I was told to make distinctions among performers. It was the intelligent, read 'grown-up,' thing to *not* like most of them, to put them down, in a witty way if you could. After a while you were lucky to like *any* performance. Was that a favor? I practically 'discriminated' myself right out of loving music. What an achievement."

William, on the other side of the desk, wasn't to be outdone. "I feel guilty, truly guilty, that we teachers do the same kind of thing from our first moment in the classroom. We walk into the room and all the students in it are on the same level, so to speak. There's a certain equality in the class. We can't have that. So we test everyone. If the tests are hard enough and frequent enough, the single level becomes a finely articulated pyramid. The 91.4 is above the 91.3. Perhaps two decimal places, perhaps three!" William stopped for a breath. "We perpetuate the humiliations Catherine remembers, and then rationalize these cruelties quite away. Our command of the language helps us in this. Our unthinking—ah, unthinking—commitments to clichés about 'excellence,' 'rigor,' and so on, help us. The hierarchized classroom is much like Eleanor's hierarchized violinists. Once, everyone who played gave her pleasure; then, with 'education,' perhaps only one violinist, alone at the pinnacle of a hierarchy, is worth listening to. Or perhaps no one! A teacher taking pride in a class without a single 'A' in the room."

"Words, books, paintings, performances; human beings. All can be hierarchized," the teacher said sadly. "The consequence is silent suffering on a breathtaking scale. Children run a race at a fair. One child wins. A crowd cheers. A camera captures the triumphant expression on the winner's face. It doesn't record what the other runners feel; *we* don't record what they feel. Some of the children are saddened in one way, some in another; some are angry; some are vengeful. 'My time will come,' the latter say, and the society-at-large approves. But all these feelings, including the victor's, are inhumane feelings. The race should not have been run."

Jerry couldn't contain his uneasiness. "How else are you going to do it? To have excellence, excuse the expression? To have a society, even? Tell me an important collective activity that works otherwise."

The teacher looked intently and compassionately at Jerry and was quiet for a moment. "When you ask for a whole society, Jerry, we can invoke the totemic world again. But as we come closer to modern times, describing an alternative becomes hard. What we've long had everywhere around us are races, winners, humiliations—hierarchies. There are strong hints, though, just before modern times, in medieval Europe."

"When I studied medieval art," Catherine said, "I couldn't help thinking that there was more in it than in the art that followed. The symbolism seemed deeper."

"Oh yes," the teacher agreed. "Take buildings. For the last several centuries they've been either convenient structures or beautiful structures, or sometimes both. But the medieval cathedral was more than merely convenient or beautiful—two categories that we tremendously over-value in modern times. The cathedral was symbolic, as you say. To be symbolic, of course, is under-valued now. You'll see why. The cathedral was a church building and it was other things at the same time, exactly like a person who remains herself and also becomes other people, cumulatively. Symbolism depended on boundary-dissolution, which was intermittently alive in medieval Europe. So the building could be experienced by ordinary people as a cathedral, as Mary, as Old Testament prophets, New Testament saints, and kings of France, even as mathematical ratios and musical intervals, all at once. The experience was totemic and often, embarrassingly often to a modern sensibility, ecstatic."

"The West had a totemic or partially totemic interlude, then?" William asked.

"I believe so," said the teacher.

"That's a material thing, the cathedral," Jerry objected. "Material things might have multiple meanings; I grant that. I want a process, a complex process."

"Then let's move to a small village near our cathedral," the teacher said. "There's a sick child in the village and many of the adults and children there are suffering for and with her. The child's mother goes to an elderly widow's house to ask her help. The old woman, wearing black—you'll guess that when the totemic period ends she'll be called a witch—goes to her basement chamber, where a large iron pot sits on a grate and bottles and trays line shelves on the walls. The basement is a cave, a womb, in the earth, the mother who never dies. Life grows in such caves. The healer takes some heavy, gray, alloyed stones and puts them in the heating pot. Then she adds precise quantities of substances from her shelves, in a prescribed order. The sick little girl is also 'heavy,' 'gray,' and 'alloyed.' When she's well, she's 'light,' 'golden,' and 'pure.' If the old woman can make her stones light, golden, and pure, and if she and the entire village believe that the child *is the stones*, then the child becomes well. A primary distinction is *un*-made between the girl and the stones, and at the same time, careful distinctions are *made* regarding the substances on the shelves. Both ways to use the mind, not one way, participate in the process, and they're guided by the fundamental kindness of healing."

"Let me assure you," said Eleanor, "that it's not the kindest people who get into medical school."

"You would have scientific research limited to projects connected to kindness?" asked Jerry.

"Absolutely," the teacher replied emphatically. "Remember that it wasn't long before that old woman would be burned at the stake. The post-totemic Renaissance only valued the distinction-making activity related to her shelves. Modernity beginning with the Renaissance kept and elaborated that activity, making it into natural science. Modernity melted down her cauldron, and called that demystification. It repudiated her ends, and called that objectivity."

"It seems like a dried-up sort of science, cut off like that from human welfare," Catherine said.

"Restoring the place of kindness and boundary-dissolution would certainly change science—and who knows what else," Eleanor added.

"Everything," the teacher said with a grin.

3.

Language

"The precision and orderliness of the healer's shelf-work sound like the way we're taught to speak and write, doesn't it?" Eleanor said. "She measured amounts of things precisely, and followed a correct order for them to be added to the pot. We define our words precisely, and we follow a correct order in stringing them together."

"The parallel is exact," the teacher said. "Precision and orderliness are the positions that distinction-makers take toward words."

"Are you implying that distinction-*un*makers take a different position toward words?" Jerry asked.

"You know, I've always thought that kind people, distinction-unmakers, talk differently, I mean *really* differently, from other people," Catherine interjected.

"And the languages totemic people spoke are quite different from most of the languages we run into nowadays," William added. "The differences may lie in alternatives to precision and orderliness. As I think about some of these languages, I believe there are indeed alternative positions."

"Look at this extremely difficult and extremely important matter this way," the teacher said. "Making distinctions among words is intended to give you a 'best' word, the most precise word for the job.

Catherine remembers this from third grade. And orderliness stands to groups of words as precision stands to words taken one at a time. Now, imagine that: as for persons, so for words. Persons between whom distinctions are un-made can enlarge. Words can enlarge in the same way. The distinction-unmaker's position toward words is *multiplicity* of meaning rather than precision, in other words singularity of meaning. My own exposure to older languages also suggests much less interest in orderliness where individual words are thick with meaning. I don't want to be too aphoristic about this, but it looks as if single-meaninged, boundary-rigid *people* go in for orderliness, and multiple-meaninged, boundary-negotiable people don't need it; single-meaninged, precise *words* go in for orderliness, multiple-meaninged words don't need it."

"Wait," Jerry interposed, looking particularly eager.

The others turned toward him, expecting an objection.

"I think I have your long answer to Eleanor's question about choosing between kindness and intelligence. You've tied kindness to words with multiple meanings, right? Catherine intuits something about this. You're surely going to tie *intelligence* to words with single meanings, and I'm pretty certain I know how you're going to do it. OK. Among the meanings of a word with a bunch of meanings is the precise one, *just as* a person becoming his loved ones is also himself. The logic of that gives you the following: the position toward multiple meanings *contains* the position toward single meanings, and not vice versa. Put another way, kindness has an intelligence of its own, intelligence has no kindness of its own."

The teacher got up from his chair, walked over to Jerry, and gripped his shoulder. Both of them beamed.

When the teacher resumed his seat, he said, "I owe Jerry how I would go about connecting precision and orderliness to what modernity calls intelligence. You'll tell us, Jerry, if it's what you thought. When words are precise and sentence-order is correct, then the legislators of intelligence tell us to use this equipment in a special way: we're to make two kinds of sentences, one termed universal, the other particular. We're then to arrange them so that a particular sentence called the conclusion is generated by the universal and particular sentences. This three-part machine made out of words—universal sentences, particular sentences, and conclusions—becomes the route to problem-solving, to prediction, to all the operations of what the legislators say intelligence is. If you can bear two kinds of examples, I'll show you what troubles this machine has brought us."

"Fire away," Eleanor said.

"The first use of the three-part machine, which of course goes by the name 'logic,' controls people; the second use controls nature, everything other than people," the teacher said. "That's everything there is, lying spread before logic to be used. The aim, notice, isn't kindness, but use. Here's a universal sentence: anybody who steals an apple that belongs to somebody else, any time, any place, is a criminal. The 'any time, any place' in the sentence are what make it universal. Add a particular sentence: at 2:40 p.m. on July 6, 1990, at the intersection of Routes 7 and 31, Robert Smith stole an apple belonging to somebody else. All of those time- and place-specifics make that sentence particular. The conclusion, which follows mechanically, is, Robert Smith is a criminal. The conduct of modern societies is based on this mechanical device. Turn quickly from society to nature, in order to see something remarkable. Here are two universal sentences: water freezes at 0 degrees Centigrade, any time, any place; when water freezes, it expands, any time, any place. A particular sentence: Mary Jones filled a bottle made of very fragile glass with water at 10 p.m. in her apartment, capped the bottle tightly, and put it in her freezer, which was set at 10 below zero Centigrade. Conclusion: the next morning she found broken glass in her freezer. If the time and date of the particulars were today, then we'd be predicting what Mary Jones will find tomorrow. We'd be predicting the future, something modernity is obsessively interested in doing. What we see in the two examples is the control of persons and of nature by way of a single, mechanical process, a very simple one. In one case, lawgivers write the universals; in the other, scientists discover the universals. Intelligence, defined as competence in logic, is devoted almost exclusively to control, use. That's what we've come to."

William was excited again. "Pre-urban communities don't seem to have been communities of laws, of the three-part language processes you describe, and they don't seem to have oriented themselves to nature as controllers. Councils, where decisions affecting the community as a whole were made, probably worked more as occasions to dissolve boundaries than to join particulars to universals in order to entail conclusions. And nature was brought into the totemic scheme; otherwise it was left alone."

"You have to agree that sometimes there's kindness in the social laws and in the scientific laws," Jerry said. "There are laws that are just, and there's science that heals. But the kindness isn't there on principle."

"Unless kindness is there all the time, on principle, we're going to slide deeper and deeper into some kind of obliviousness, like a machine's obliviousness," Catherine said gloomily.

"Let's get a breath of air," Eleanor said.

The teacher and his friends walked outside into the vegetable garden. There were no rows and paths there; the teacher had thrown an apron-full of all kinds of seed into the air on the first windy morning after thaw, then moved some of them an inch here or a foot there, on his hands and knees, for an hour or two every subsequent morning for a couple of weeks. A riot of food was the result. When he was asked what his method was those mornings crawling over the garden, he replied that it was when he had given up method that the seeds let him know where they wanted to be.

4.

Play

The five were back at the kitchen table. Catherine had been preoccupied in the garden. "I was trying to think how kind people talked," she said. "I think that good mothers do it when they talk to their babies. The words are funny, too. The mother and baby are making nonsensical, or more-than-sensical, sounds, and they're laughing. They're playing. I think that's the model of kind talk. It feels like the absolute opposite of a machine."

"Grandmothers like me can see it twice in our lives," Eleanor said. "When we're mothers we're participants and we might not know or be able to verbalize what's going on, but when we're grandmothers and we see our kids with their kids, we have distance, and there it is. What Catherine describes is the talk that persuades a new human being that the world is good. I agree with you, Catherine. Loving moms and their babies set the pattern. Loving dads too if they're OK."

"It's not a pattern that's carried very far into adulthood, is it?" Jerry said. "It would be—interesting—if law-school professors patted their students on the head and called them their pootchie-pies."

"I think sometimes that you're feeding me lines, Jerry," the teacher said laughing. "You want me to say your law-school professors should do just that. To oblige you, and, incidentally, because it's as true as trees grow up not down, I will: professors should often talk and act like loving mothers with babies. More, and better still: students should behave in the same way toward their professors! Many of the ways in which people can be kind to each other should be playful, full of laughter. Don't loving mothers become their babies, hence their talk, and don't babies become their mothers, hence their security and happiness? Don't we want this for everyone?"

"I'm going to cry," Catherine said, smiling.

"Cry," the teacher said, also smiling.

"It's quite a picture," William said. "We'd be playing much of the time. On the other hand, this may be what we're for, so to speak."

"Hmm," from Jerry.

"The adult world is by-and-large so solemn, so self-absorbed and calculating; there is no way to describe it that catches the immensity and inanity of it," the teacher said. "It's like the suffering of the many millions who don't win the world's races, races that should not be run. But the unhappiness can be addressed. We only have to be careful not to be solemn, or self-absorbed, or, what did I say, calculating, about it. We could start with waltzing. It's a direct connection to small children worldwide."

"I'll bite. How?" Jerry asked.

"Children love to spin. Wherever you go, you see toddlers spinning, falling down, and giggling. When they grow up, they're inclined to choose damaging ways to duplicate this dizziness. Now waltzing is none other than two spinning adults, each keeping the other from falling down. They do this to pleasant music in three-quarter time. A marvelous activity."

Jerry scratched his head, posing. "We've got teachers and students speaking nonsense syllables to each other . . ."

". . .and singing them," the teacher interrupted.

". . .and singing them," Jerry went on, "I presume during the day, and at night they, and everybody else, waltz."

"You're coming right along," the teacher said.

"Spinning reminds me of something," Eleanor said. "By the way, the picture you're drawing is affecting me the same as Catherine. I'm old and about as illusion-free as they come, but when I imagine that world, the tears come. Anyway, spinning. Some smart work in a hospital near mine twenty years ago intimated that infants who aren't moved around enough, rocked, say, can suffer lifelong difficulty feeling pleasure. The big payoff of the work was that such difficulties were probably factors in these infants-become-men doing violence on others. I thought about that a lot. More is involved, of course, but still, rocking kids might stop some adult violence later. I wonder if adults rocking themselves might stop some violence."

The teacher stood up slowly. "To borrow a classical expression, Eureka, Eleanor. Our waltzing population comes in pairs. We need physical activities for people when they're alone. In honor of Eleanor, we today introduce the grown-up rocking horse in every home. We devise a simple pattern, so that people can make them themselves. Five feet long, possibly two-and-a-half feet high, and heavy. People will rock their troubles away every night."

"Singing nonsense songs on their rocking horses." Jerry's tone unexpectedly lacked its earlier edge.

"Nonsense songs, cowgirl songs, cowboy songs if there are any, grand opera," Catherine crooned.

"That happiness might displace violence is an age-old dream," William said, shaking his head. "Can play, tenderness, kindness prevail in a blood-soaked world?"

"Yes," the teacher said simply.

"The blood-soaked world," Jerry repeated, the light gone out of his eyes. "We Americans are naive. Why not; we have oceans on two sides of us and we're rich. But the rest of the world knows. Life is hard, often terrible. And here we are, fantasizing to make ourselves feel good in a sylvan hideaway."

A severe expression passed over the teacher's face. He closed his eyes tightly for a moment, opened them, and the severity was gone. But he spoke rapidly and forcefully. "There is not a shadow of frivolity in what we're discussing, Jerry. Nothing of the kind. It's because of the world's suffering that we must begin from new axioms—or as William surmises, very old axioms that were coercively replaced with the coming of cities by less human, cruel, axiom-like claims. Human beings are not meant to work themselves or each other to death, or to create death-in-life for each other and call it virtue, or to kill each other with industrial efficiency. We're meant to help each other and the world, to become each other and the world, to laugh, eat, make love, even babble, waltz, and rock. We work, to make things and to grow food. Do you think I work hard in the garden? First, it's not even work. With my face six inches from the soil, ideas come to me, music comes. I help feed three families in the village; there's that much food. We aren't with the earth correctly, Jerry, a tremendous and fixable problem. Between that fact, and the insane hierarchical economic, political, and social arrangements built by stunningly few half-people five thousand years ago and sustained by their successors since, the human world has become pathetic in rich places and tragic in poor ones. It's our responsibility every moment of our lives to try to reverse this course. Since human beings have only recently done these things to themselves, and since all babies are sane, and since in the distant past probably most adults were sane too, for more generations than we've been crazy, this course can be reversed."

"What makes me mad," Eleanor said after a time, "is that there's so much *phony* play going on. It's like those races with mostly losers. There are games everywhere you look, but they're games that ape the hierarchies, or staff them with more half-people. What you get is phony happiness, a kind of mean-spirited glee at having triumphed over somebody."

"The mean-spiritedness is extremely serious," the teacher said, "Young boys are brought up to admire a version of male adulthood that's tied to those phony games. Boys learn to cooperate on teams in order to defeat other teams, a perversion of the aims of cooperation. The terrible, but historically correct, analogy is to soldiers cooperating in order to kill enemy soldiers. So the worst is brought out in boys, and in a society that keeps boys from maturing properly, compassionately, the consequences are appalling—especially appalling for women and children. And still we applaud sports figures, as if they've achieved something humanly significant. Sport has much to answer for."

"Many people claim to love sport," William said, "but I don't believe they love sport so much as they love to win at sport, as Eleanor suggests. Winning is the opposite of playing. I used to play tennis, an innocent enough game compared to the patently brutal ones, and I used what skill I possessed to put the ball where the other player—my opponent, my enemy—couldn't hit it. That meant that I didn't love to play tennis, I loved to win at tennis. If I had really loved to play, I'd have put the ball where the other person *could* hit it, and the volley would have gone on and on. I'd have sufficiently *been* the other person to know what he could and couldn't return."

"A player out to win might also adjust his boundaries in order to know what the other player can and can't do," Jerry said, "but he would use the knowledge another way. An example of distinction-unmaking to the wrong end?"

"Yes," the teacher said.

"You know, there are no-winners-no-losers games," Catherine said. "That would make things easier. I have a book describing a bunch of them. My children play them all and have a terrific time."

"The people who invent such games should win the famous international prizes," the teacher said. "They wouldn't accept them, but they should win them."

"They should win, and the great cook-book writers should win, and no one else. Imagine inventing desserts that sweep away your woes for a little while." Eleanor licked her lips.

"I think we have universal agreement about the prize-win—I mean prize-deservers," the teacher said.

"Are we allowed to say 'universal'?" Jerry asked solemnly, smiling.

"This once," the teacher said grandly.

5.

Time

"It looks as if words can be empty or nearly empty—one meaning is close to empty—or they can be full; and as if people can be empty or nearly empty, or they can be full," Jerry said. "Words and people. Anything else?"

"Moments," the teacher said.

"Moments can be empty or full?" Jerry asked. "Aren't they just...moments? You can do something interesting at a particular moment, or lie around empty-headed at a particular moment; I can see that. But you mean something different."

Catherine joined in animatedly. "I could swear that there are moments with clay or with my chisels when time changes its character. It isn't that it 'flies' or anything like that: time is somehow different, and better. Sometimes with my children, too."

"Perhaps we have privileged activities," William said, "that briefly re-make time."

"I don't disparage such experiences; I seek them out too," the teacher said, "but they're not exactly what I mean by full moments. What I mean is actually distant from our experience. At least it has been in modern times. Do you remember when we were talking about universal sentences and particular sentences, and the machine control of people and nature? Odd as it sounds, time itself falls prey to that machine."

"I can see the application of mechanical logic to the law—I sure hope I can see it by now—and to science, but you've lost me," Jerry said. "Logic and *time*?"

Eleanor, Catherine, and William also looked puzzled.

"The question of time goes deep," the teacher said. "That's why modern society shrugs it off by supplying us with calendars and watches, adding, if necessary, that time is simply a given. Then modernity gets on with what it thinks are accessible matters, like politics, and art. One mistake on top of another. We need to stop, and take on the question of time from scratch. Let's say you've drawn a time-line, like the ones you occasionally see in popular histories. There's a point on such a line representing the present. To the left of that point is the past, to the right the future."

"Like a number line with negative numbers to the left of zero and positive numbers to the right, right?" Jerry said.

"Exactly. Now, regarding the past-segment of the line, you mark off years, and locate events at this point or that point. The longer ago the event, the farther to the left. At the point '1789,' for example, you can locate the French Revolution. All of these points can in fact have a particular sentence like, 'In 1789, in France, a revolution occurred,' associated with them. Are we together?"

Nods from the group.

"*Universal* sentences, though, would have to be above the line; they would have to apply to all the points on the line, bar none. It begins to appear as if we have two parts of our three-part thought-machine before us: a few universal sentences hovering over the time-line, and a great many particular sentences, a thick chronicle, making up the line. So where's the conclusion, the third part and payoff, I ask rhetorically? Well, you make note of several particular events in France in 1788, 1787, and perhaps earlier. You posit universals like, 'At all times in all places, revolutions occur if'—you fill in the blank. As we know, parenthetically, no way to fill in blanks like that has ever held up; but social scientists need to make a living. Anyway, you put the right 1788-and-earlier particular sentences together with the right universal sentences, and voilà, you have the French Revolution, your conclusion. The three parts of the machine are locked up tight. As many teachers are in the habit of saying, you've learned something."

"But you already know there was a French Revolution," Eleanor objected.

"Very observant, Eleanor," the teacher said. "You know the French Revolution happened. Isn't that convenient? This prediction of something you already know happened is sometimes technically called an 'explanation.' What we need to notice is that the three-stage mental operation that we've observed controlling people and controlling nature also has much to do with the activity called 'learning from the past.' I'll go farther. It also has much to do with the activity called 'planning for the future.'"

"Hard going," Eleanor said.

"It's hard, but clear," from Catherine.

The teacher resumed. "About planning for the future: say we write particular sentences not for points in the past, but for points clustered in the present. 'Right now, in London, such and such is happening.' 'Right now, in New York, this and that are happening.' The universal sentences are the same as before, suspended nobly over the whole line, past, present, and future. But, with the particular sentences in the present and the universal sentences applicable everywhere, where will the conclusions go? They have to fall to the right of the particular sentences on the time-line, so they won't appear in the past, where the conclusions associated with learning were to be found; they'll fall in the future. It doesn't occur to us that the main reason we even plot a future may be to contain conclusions, the third and completing elements of the ubiquitous machine. Those conclusions are predictions, and we know how important predicting the future is to societies addicted to control. Our conclusion, following from the London and New York particulars and the universals given to us by social science, might be that a particular international business deal is going to be made. You'll next act accordingly, waiting confidently for the deal you've predicted, or if you don't want it to go through, doing something to block it. Either way, you've planned, and you've done it via the same mental operations you invoked when you learned."

"There's something elegant in that, isn't there?" Jerry asked.

"Yes," the teacher replied. "If you believe elegance to be a first-class good, you've achieved something remarkable with this symmetry of learning from the past and planning for the future. And don't forget controlling people and nature. I want to point out the costs of the symmetry. A person has so much mental energy in a day. It's a finite amount. Modern people are asked to put a good deal of that finite energy into learning and planning, aren't they? That's practically what being intelligent is about, we're told, along with making distinctions and solving problems. So energy goes to the past and energy goes to the future. What's left goes to the present, which, it's crucial to remember, is when we're concretely living. Very often what's left for the present isn't much. An empty present-moment results. It's this emptiness that's the equivalent of an empty word and an empty person in a distinction-making society."

"When we sought out instances of full persons and full words, we looked at the totemic world, where distinctions can be dissolved," William said. "That must be where we find full moments."

"Yes," the teacher said, "there. Those people—all of us, before cities came—did not habitually resort to the three-part machine, hence the absence of the lust to control people and nature. Their not relying on the machine also means—observe what this explains of travelers' accounts of totemic peoples—that first, these peoples don't learn from the past, and second, they don't plan for the future. Both things are indeed true of them. Haven't unsympathetic travelers consistently called such people stupid, since there could be no question in most modern minds that smart people learn and plan continuously? Three considerations must be brought forward. One, totemic peoples don't *need* to learn the way we learn and plan the way we plan. In fact they barely acknowledge the existences of a past to learn from or a future to plan for. Totemic societies are so stable—for the unsympathetic, again, repetitive, uncreative—that they don't require the careful tactics toward the past and future that novelty-ridden modern societies do. Two, with little or no mental energy going to the past and to the future in the totemic world, most or all of it is available for the present moment. *This* is the full moment, the one I said was remote from us. Sympathetic travelers to totemic places remark on how completely present their hosts seem to them. And three, with no future to plan and re-plan for unceasingly, totemic peoples are less afraid to die. One's death can only come in the future, after all. The more I work up the future and think about it, the more my inevitable death, the future's most poignant feature, weighs on me. Don't unusually intelligent modern people and cultures like the classical Greek and Renaissance high cultures, seem to fear death more than others? They do; they must. By contrast, the full moments of logic-free time are relieved of death-terror."

"Wow," from Catherine and Eleanor simultaneously.

"How can we have such moments?" Jerry asked.

"We return to how we can enlarge ourselves, and live correctly with each other and with nature," the teacher replied. "We restore our capacity for boundary-dissolution-at-will. We bring distinction-unmaking into parity with distinction-making, embracing the whole of mental life, no longer calling half of it the whole. Then we entirely naturally move toward full personhood, toward a language of full words, and toward full moments. I should add that the freedom from death-terror of full moments returns us to the very beginning of our conversation. It's possible to say now that the life we talked about can be lived in full time, from which the fear of death has been lifted, and which needs no glamor or acquisitions or heroism to feel complete. This rather than life in empty time, increasingly death-haunted, increasingly felt as incomplete. The two ways are worlds apart."

William said, "Your argument not only explains why so many travelers to remote places patronized the totemic peoples they encountered, but why, personally, I cared so much and in such confusion for many of my least accomplished students. Of course there were always accomplished students, by the school's and the society's standards: expert in learning, in planning, in distinction-making and problem-solving. I had no difficulty liking them. But at one period especially, there seemed to have erupted from our efficiency society a number of dreamy young men and women who were expert in none of these things, but to whom our hearts went out. Not that they were totemic. What they shared with totemic peoples was an absence of investment in learning and planning. What they did not seem to have was the completeness of mental life that filled their present moments: they weren't distinction-dissolvers, but broken distinction-makers. Their present moments were nearly as empty as their pasts and futures, and their efforts to fill them were too often self-deceived or self-destructive, or both. I believe we felt so strongly about them because now and then they looked like totemic adolescents right in our stuffy adult midst, and because we knew that they weren't. Fondness, perhaps yearning, and pity were mixed in an unusual alloy for a teacher. It's clearer to me now."

"My experience was the same," the teacher said, sighing. "I wanted those kids to have the full moments that their empty pasts and futures implied, but they didn't have them, and I grieved for them. The society plucked them for its purposes, just as it plucked the achievers."

"Remember that those sweet dummies had a stronger moral sense than most of the adult world," Catherine said with heat. "I was one of them, and my friends and I did something about injustices in this society that the logic choppers were too constipated to do. And not all of us were bought off."

The teacher looked pained. "I apologize, Catherine. I shouldn't have spoken in such general terms. The broken distinction-making William referred to had surprising results. We were with you then, and perhaps the way we spoke just now comes from our disappointment, in many of your friends and in ourselves, that the best of those results weren't longer-lived. But you certainly were not bought off, and I should have spoken more carefully."

"I ask your forgiveness too," William said.

Catherine got up from her chair, walked around to William's place, and kissed him on the forehead. The teacher squeezed both her hands.

6.

Music

"Something occurs to me," Eleanor said. "The real play William describes, going on over a long time, and the full moments we've been talking about, remind me of music. I remember reading a French anthropologist, maybe thirty years ago, who said that the one mystery of the human condition was music. He thought, if I remember right, that myth was the sustaining mental food of human beings for thousands of years, and when myth was disallowed—was that when the distinction-dissolving half of mind was disallowed, in the first cities?—music took its place. Fugue, I think he said, took the place of myth. Boy, we must be starved these days."

"Starved indeed," William said. "You remember clearly, Eleanor. I quite agree with your French anthropologist. I'll tell you a story. Early in my career I thought that certain anthropological and psychoanalytic notions could be woven together. There were dark corners I hoped a synthesis of the two disciplines might illuminate somewhat. Not much came of it, but I did come to know several psychoanalysts fairly well. One conversation, with a renowned training analyst, remained with me vividly—like your passage about myth and fugue, Eleanor. My friend was visiting campus on the eve of his retirement from practice. He seemed distracted as we spoke into the night. Finally he looked at me peculiarly, in dismay, but in a dismay that accompanied a deep insight, a discovery. He said that he had come to believe that the best route to personal integration the West had found wasn't psychoanalytic treatment, but the daily discipline and joy of string-quartet playing. He thought that two or three years of intensive lessons on the violin, viola, or cello, followed by playing quartets every night, indefinitely, would do more good than a lifetime of psychoanalysis. I've never forgotten his tone of voice, his strange excitement. The mystery of music, the life-serving mystery."

"That must have cost him a good deal to tell you," Eleanor said. "Think what he was retiring from doing."

"The string quartets of Haydn, Mozart, Beethoven and Brahms, with the fugues of Bach, are the glory of the West," the teacher said. "They're food for mind, and they heal. They aren't enough: a person must first be able to become another, to do no harm. Then, nothing builds on that foundation like great music, and it builds mysteriously."

Catherine became excited again. "I'm a visual person, I guess, but I can't live without Beethoven's late quartets, period. I have a way of thinking about them that fits a little into what we're talking about. I imagine that the mind works two ways, producing horizontal lines, like those time-lines or like melodies in a musical score, and producing vertical lines, maybe like full moments or like the harmonies in a score. That way the mind actually *looks* like a string-quartet score: four horizontal, melodic lines, plus hundreds and hundreds of vertical harmonies, practically at every note. When you listen hard to a great quartet, you're listening to horizontal and vertical events that are happening simultaneously. That's the whole mind you're hearing, and *your* whole mind is stimulated into activity. All your lights switch on. If you're *playing* in a quartet, it's even better; the lights glow brighter and brighter."

"That's great, Catherine," Jerry said equally excited. "Could we listen to a late Beethoven together?"

"I'd like nothing better," Catherine said, glowing.

"What a fine way to see and hear a quartet, Catherine," the teacher said. "The musical quality of the melodies and harmonies keeps the listener continuously enmeshed in those simultaneous horizontal and vertical events. If you play, the technical challenges of your part go a step further to keep you concentrated: who could think of anything else while playing a Beethoven cello part? Some people believe that great melodies hold us because they create anticipations of closed, complete experiences, aural ones, and we await the closures with eager pleasure. Some people believe that great melodies have to do with the shapes of brain circuits. Whatever it is that's happening—it remains a mystery to me—between the birth of Bach and the death of Brahms, a few composers gave a culture that insists on celebrating only the virtuosity of half-people, nourishing and healing examples of wholeness."

"Brahms died before 1900," Jerry said. "What does that mean about the twentieth century?"

The teacher grimaced. "Not much of a century for music—a damning judgment on a century, isn't it? There was some music, in Russia, France, in the first half of the century. A few popular-song writers in America. But the popular music of the second half of the century has done a remarkable thing. If you don't mind a psychoanalytic judgment, this music has released destructive material in the young, and not cathartically. We've seen the conscious promotion of regression in the service not of health, but of illness. It's an unprecedented and terrible phenomenon. Coupled with television, which promotes similar regressions, also in the interest of profits, popular music has done considerable harm to an already damaged, if rich, West."

"Popular-music moguls probably fool around with kids' boundaries the way we were saying some athletes—or generals, or businessmen—fuse with their opponents in order to defeat them," Jerry said. "They sound to me like the most scientific of all the proponents of boundary-dissolution-in-order-to-get-the-other-guy, advertising executives."

"Look at television and popular music—both fueled by advertising," Eleanor said. "An unholy trio. They have as much to answer for as sport."

"Great music isn't faring well in such a climate," the teacher said sadly. "A poor century for Bach."

"A toast to Bach, then," William said.

The teacher brightened. The friends lifted imaginary wine-glasses.

"To Bach," from all.

7.

Education

"I attended a reading at the university recently," William said, "at the end of which someone asked the quite well-known poet who he thought the greatest poet who had ever lived was. I expected an answer like Homer or Milton or Shakespeare. The poet unhesitatingly answered, 'Bach.' I'd add 'teacher' to poet."

"So would I," the teacher said.

"Teachers," Catherine said angrily. "Most of us know teachers only in schoolrooms, where the distinction-making you described, William, rewards some kids and punishes others—hurts all of them. I don't mean it to sound as rotten as it sounds, but at least Bach is dead."

"It's not so rotten, Catherine," the teacher said. "Many of our true teachers are dead. We read them or hear their music or look at what they've made in a special kind of privacy. And many of the living true teachers are people's grandmothers who've worked their farms instead of going to school, let alone teaching in school. You won't get any argument about schoolrooms from us."

"But they have to be argued about in some way or other: so many kids are committed to them—as in committing the people we decide are unfit for society to mental institutions. But they're our own kids!"

Eleanor lowered her voice. "My two boys went to school. Their kids are going to school."

"Schools can be fixed," Jerry insisted. "They're not going to disappear, so they *have* to be fixed."

"Look at where we are," Eleanor continued. "Boys have bad adult models—aggressive men wherever the boys look, plus small-scale contests, big-time contests, some men rich and powerful, most men failures at all that, and mad about it their whole lives. Too many men are predators, by one definition or another, on women. Boys are wallowing in this muck, in psychotic music, in television that's insulting to women, to intelligence. We haven't even *talked* about girls. For one thing, they're in school with these very boys. They're all, girls and boys together, in the same adult male world and the same idiotic popular culture. Maybe girls have a slightly better chance of growing up to be women than boys have to be men, maybe not. But they're both a long way from being *helped* to become substantial human beings."

"I don't mean to question what you feel about how things are," Jerry said, "but don't you think that so many years at the hospital might have predisposed you to seeing the whole society around the hospital as sick?"

Catherine said, "Part of it is the difference between being a man or a woman in the society, Jerry. Eleanor may be especially sensitive to what's wrong because of her life in nursing, and there may be a lot that's right. But what you have to understand is that it's men who pretty much define what's right. Don't men say professional sports are right? Women are in a better position to judge the weight of what's wrong, and I tell you, Jerry, too much is wrong."

"I can accept that, I think," Jerry said.

"Too much is wrong," the teacher repeated. "Eleanor misses very little. So let's begin. How should schools be, in the face of what Eleanor describes?"

"The classroom must not be hierarchized," William began.

"End tests?" asked Jerry.

"End them," William said. "A room occupied by human beings of whatever age, who are equal and becoming fuller, not ranked and becoming emptier."

"How about mixing up the kids' ages and giving them all things to do other than sitting on their behinds?" Eleanor said.

"Fourteen-year-olds can be given six-year-olds to take care of," Catherine said. "They can take care of animals and plants together, right in school. That will help them preserve what ability to become others they still have, and build new capacity for it. I identified with two pet rabbits so completely when I was in first and second grade that I began to hop as soon as I was out of the classroom. They saved my sanity."

"Wonderful," the teacher said. "If there have to be schools, let them be as you say. The children and the adults with them can also learn to make important things, like clothes, with their hands. They can cook good big lunches at noon and take a long time to eat them. School can be the time for learning dozens of songs from all over the world, and dances, and stories. Think what celebrations the schools can have, with food, music, dancing, and stories. For the whole time in school, an equilibrium of distinction-making and distinction-dissolving activities would be maintained, so the young would be whole and strong at the end of their schooling."

"We teachers are fanatics about curriculum, it goes without saying," William added. "I would promote the learning of a totemic language throughout this splendid schooling. There are difficulties, of course, since most of them are gone—it's not too much to say 'killed,' by civilized encroachment."

"Of course, William," the teacher said. "I'm fond of Middle Egyptian, myself. Children take to it because of the drawing and color. There's also a very good Egyptian grammar available, published in England. One of the glories of hieroglyphics is the clarity of their depiction of boundary-dissolution and doubling. If a human being is to be shown possessing all human and all, say, raptor attributes, you simply make a drawing of a person with a hawk's head. What could be more straightforward? If the hawk happens to have several stories associated with it, in all likelihood featuring even more boundary-dissolutions, the reader of the drawing will receive the stories. All of this in one hieroglyph."

"A feature of Egyptian hieroglyphs that charms me," William said, "is that they're often silent. We don't know how to pronounce the ones that can be spoken, and there's reason to believe that many of them aren't to be spoken at all. Our writing systems are tied to speech. The letters of alphabets cue spoken sounds. Middle Egyptian is tied to thought, not speech—a larger world."

"Whole-thinking, you're arguing?" Jerry said.

"I believe so," William replied.

"Then Middle Egyptian it is," Catherine said, "along with sewing, carving, cooking, waltzing, the cha cha, the trepak, rocking horses, singing in choruses, telling and listening to stories, reading novels, playing recorders in all registers. I want to go to that school!"

"Wait a second," Jerry said. "We said equilibrium, right? Where's mathematics, the sciences? Woops: the sciences insofar as they're devoted to humane ends."

"Let's have them," the teacher said. "Mathematics and symbolic logic can be taught as brilliant adventures in distinction-making. One of the more ironic aspects of the strangle-hold distinction-making has on the schools is that its quality is poor. 'Sloppy distinction-making' doesn't sound right. There are fine materials in the foundations of mathematics, though, that children would thrive on, just as they would thrive on Middle Egyptian. *There's* equilibrium. Let's have the strongest possible distinction-making experiences set in the strongest possible context of expressive, practical, fanciful, distinction-dissolving happiness. How can the adult world do less for its children?"

"And if schools won't go our way?" Jerry asked. "They aren't likely to, as we all know."

"We do know it, but we keep the pressure on them anyway," Eleanor said resolutely.

"In most places a few adults can start a school of their own," Catherine said. "Three college friends of mine did that for ten years.

They ran a secret play-group masquerading as an elementary school, for six to ten-year-olds, in a church annex. What they told the state was one thing, what the kids did once the doors were closed was another. My daughter went there its last year, so I had a chance to see how the long-timers at the school were doing. The ten-year-olds were spunky—I'd say unusually so—and happy. And they only did a few of the things we've been talking about."

"There's nothing wrong with taking kids out of school altogether if there isn't a place like Catherine's friends' school around," Eleanor said. "Keep the pressure on existing schools, public and private; start our own small schools; and home-school—all three. A few parents can get together and home-school in something like the way Catherine's friends schooled in a church space, but in people's living-rooms and on walks in the park. Why not?"

"Why not?" the teacher said.

"What about the inroads of bad models and the pop culture?" Jerry asked.

"Then *we* must be aggressive," the teacher said. "If we have to take our children to other places, where these influences are weaker, then we must relegate thoughts of career to a subordinate position and do just that. It will usually mean leaving the city. That cannot come as a surprise. Once again we come to rejecting cities on principle, escaping their hysteria and their superficiality represented as glamor or culture. Wherever we are, we can not have television, period. We should undoubtedly use automobiles much less than we do. Hackneyed as it may appear to cynics, we must go back to the land. We fill our houses with books and music, and we put our houses among plants and animals."

"This house," Eleanor said softly.

"Our school," William echoed.

8.

Domesticity

"What seems a harder problem to me, even harder than the problem of educational arrangements, is what to do about child rearing," Jerry said. "If modern institutions are really cutting our kids in half, then what about the first years at home, under that venerable institution called marriage, when kids are most susceptible? I'm not married, but most of my friends are. You're interested in contests? Courtrooms are amateur theatricals compared with what goes on in living rooms. And undoubtedly in bedrooms. Two unready or under-developed parents can't do the subtle things we're talking about, identifying and pushing away the junk in the society, inviting in or creating the good stuff, and doing it all cheerfully whatever else is going on. Impossible."

"And parents are worse than schools: they *always* think they're doing fine," Eleanor said. "Most of us are incapable of seeing how little we're doing, or how wrong we're doing what we do."

"Try telling a mother shouting at her child in a supermarket to stop it," Catherine added. "The customers will glare at *you,* not her."

"We make the mistake of believing that we live in a youth culture," William said. "Not at all. Our middle-aged men and women, terrified of dying, want to be mistaken for youth themselves. They behave like adolescents in consequence. The advertisers Jerry dislikes both exploit and go on to increase this pathos. In the African villages where I lived long ago, a birth was celebrated, expansively celebrated, for many days. Children were virtually worshipped. I had not seen such joy in the relations between adults and children before, and I've not seen it since."

"Perhaps the situation of childrearing is similar in one respect to the situation of education," the teacher said. "William refers to a clan, not a married couple alone, raising children. We must remember that the members of William's clan may be more whole-minded than we are, so we can't simply imagine a group of modern related adults calling itself a clan behaving like William's friends in Africa. Now, in the case of education, first, no formal institution at all is best, so long as the parents home-schooling their children are whole people; second, an informal institution founded by a few such parents is next best; and third, a reformed formal institution, brought into equilibrium, is next. In the case of childrearing, a clan of whole people is surely best. Young children have too much energy to be overseen by one or two adults only. And as Eleanor said, high-energy adolescents ought to be playing with them and watching over them. Second, some clan-*like* group, of whole but unrelated people, might be constituted to raise children. And third, a married couple, aware of modernity's motives and aiming at wholeness, would be much better than what we have. In both cases, education and the childrearing setting prior to it, the closer to first choices we can come, the better."

"That second possibility for childrearing is unclear to me," Jerry said.

"I have an idea about it." Catherine was flushed. "Listen to this. Say you're a woman married to a guy who turns out to have been fun to be with while a husband only, early on, but shows himself to be a poor father after a child is born—inattentive, and at the same time preoccupied with power, power over you, which you hadn't noticed before, and definitely power over the child. Not an unusual situation."

"You're not kidding," Eleanor said.

"So you divorce him, period," Catherine resumed. "No drawn-out efforts to change him, 'for the child's sake.' Grown-ups don't change so easily. For the child's real sake, you discontinue a stressed, unhappy way of life. Children oughtn't be subjected to that. But you don't remain alone. *You find other mothers just like you.*"

"And you make a—what—clan-like group of unrelated whole people to raise the kids? Mothers who have the sense to relieve themselves of jerks, and are probably boundary-dissolved for their kids, so maybe moving toward being whole," Jerry said. "I like it."

Catherine stood up and began to pace. "Four or five women who love their children too much to subject them to their husbands rent a big Victorian house together. Those places are too big for single families anyway. At any one time, say two of the mothers work in the economy, the women who *want* to work. Three mothers are home, with the six or seven or whatever number children. Among the three women at home there'll be enough range—enough spread of energy-levels, of readiness to play, of personality-types—for the children always to be with someone who genuinely wants to be with them. The mothers and the children would launch all the activities we said education was to be about. They would grow together—you know, all grow, like trees, and together, not separately; and boundary-dissolution; all that. As the mothers worked out the details of living in the house, more sharing would come about. They take turns in the economy. One good piano sits in the big room instead of several cheap pianos in separate households. It isn't a clan, but it might be a place where children could stay whole and adults could get whole again. It would sure be better than Jerry's argumentative nuclear families."

"I think some dolphins raise their children that way," Jerry said. "Not the piano—the multiple mothers without many fathers around."

"That makes a multiple-mother household plausible to me," Eleanor said. "Dolphins know what they're doing."

"Mothers unite. Mothers' groups unite, " the teacher proclaimed, smiling. "Mothers united in still larger groups might do something about television and computers and tens of thousands of deaths per year by automobile. Such a political force would do much good for the world."

"I can see young girls and boys, and adolescents helping, and the mothers; but I can't see the grown men in this," Jerry said.

"Some are in good nuclear families," Catherine said.

"I can understand both Jerry's approval of Catherine's idea and his curiosity about the place of men," William said. "We thought at one point that the mystery of the human condition might be totemism, and at another point, music. In a different sense, the mystery, the problem, of the human condition may be the place of men. We need only remember the wars and the domestic cruelties of high civilization."

"The problem is most sharply visible, and perhaps easiest to diagnose, at the Persian Gulf five thousand years ago, when civilization begins," the teacher said. "There, at the turning point of human affairs on the planet, a small number of men, possibly scouts looking for new village-sites, changed nearly everything about how we live that could be changed. Very quickly, clan-kinship, which was synonymous with society itself, was broken up into nuclear families, which had no social force, and replaced by bureaucracies, which had all the social force—the bureaucratic political and economic organizations we mistakenly believe are inevitable. The power relations Catherine discovers in small, unhappy families were installed there on the largest scale. Small numbers of men, again, created hierarchies and subhierarchies and vied to occupy their highest strata, looking down at other men, at all women and children, and at nature. The places men still want are on those high strata. They aren't good places, for men or anyone else."

"If the hierarchies were gradually collapsed to single planes, men's places would be with everyone else, right?" Jerry said. "Eventually no distinctions."

"Then we could have new groupings, men beside rather than above women and children, as you say, Jerry, all capable of the boundary-dissolutions that permit the addition of other selves to one's own self," the teacher said.

"Until then," Catherine said, "maybe mothers in small groups raising children and helping each other, and groups of mothers' groups trying to humanize the society. To the degree that happened—society de-hierarchizing, the teeth of schooling, advertising, and the rest pulled—men would be invited in, and to that degree they would accept the invitations, I think."

Catherine returned to her chair.

9.

Politics

"From households to politics, Catherine," Eleanor said. "Quite a move."

"A big jump from federations of mothers' groups to real government, I know," Catherine said. "I'm not sure how the one gets to the other."

"We could imagine a demographic solution, or at least beginning," the teacher said. "Can we assume that part of your humanizing of the society encourages people to leave cities? Numbers of small towns would grow somewhat, and many towns would be founded. These would be agricultural towns—not commercial agriculture, but garden agriculture, seeing first to self-sufficiency. Smaller numbers of people, secure in their food, would find political self-rule natural, I suspect."

"Economic self-sufficiency and political self-rule have a symmetrical feel," Jerry said.

"A well-precedented symmetry," commented William.

"I remember your mentioning to us that many of the towns of eighteenth-century France, economically pretty close to self-sufficient but ruled politically from Paris, picked up local rule without much fuss during the period of revolutionary confusion in Paris," Eleanor said addressing the teacher. "Neither the old kings nor the new democrats could have *that,* so the towns were clamped down on at the first possible moment. So much for democracy."

"We forget that all modern political systems are hierarchical, Eleanor, democracies no less than absolute monarchies, constitutional monarchies, and socialisms," the teacher said. "They're all calculative political-economic systems—as in systems theory—conjured up by distinction-makers. Some are more just than others, but they're all flawed because they neither derive from whole-thinking nor promote it."

"That's why people get confused when democracies become such empty-headed societies, I guess," Catherine said. "They're supposed to be the best people can do, not violent and not trivial, and they turn out to be both."

"Inescapable," the teacher said.

"So the point of your tens of thousands of small towns will be that they do promote whole-thinking," William said.

"Yes," the teacher said. "Self-rule among half-people often requires intervention from a central power in order to prevent gross local injustice. And that's in fortunate times, when power *has* some sense of justice. It's a dilemma as long as we don't have whole people. When we do, it isn't a dilemma: whole people can, must, be left alone."

"How will politics and economics work in towns of whole people?" asked Catherine.

"My first response would be that since these townspeople use their minds completely, they'll know what arrangements to make; they won't need to be told. Whole people can be trusted in their complicated and changing situations. Half-people, no matter how developed, or over-developed, they are in the distinction-making half of their minds, can't be trusted whatever their situations."

"Any guesses about good arrangements?" Jerry asked.

"I think they would form councils with some frequency," the teacher mused. "When a group decision needed to be made, people would get together, but not to discuss and vote: that's the democracy the classical Greeks, as one-sided a society as the world has seen, invented for us. Majorities of half-people are often wrong. How could it be otherwise? Minorities of such people often plan revenge on losing a vote. It's a reflex among half-people, like competing. That behavior is far from good enough. Our townspeople would call councils in order to dissolve the boundaries among them. They wouldn't 'discuss'; they would tell stories, nap, picnic—do what whole people like to do, with the objective of coming to a decision as one body, one person with many heads and twice that many feet."

"That may resemble the kinship politics of some neolithic communities," William remarked.

"I think so too," the teacher said. "Individual persons would matter politically in a complementary way: one person would probably prove adept over a long time at planting and harvesting potatoes and carrots, and she would always be consulted on that score. People are good at every sort of thing, and they acquire a natural authority concerning their particular competencies—not concerning everything under the sun; that's a modern absurdity—as years pass. Many judgments might be made on these grounds. Over all, we would trust that whole people would make sure that everyone ate well, and was warm in the winter, and that every provision for a full life would be made."

"You have a lot of faith in them," Eleanor said.

"Many years ago, when I was young, I wondered about war and starvation and everyday meanness, and I asked myself if I were doomed to regard human beings as failed creatures, a mistake in nature, sometimes wonderful in one way or another, but often despicable," the teacher said. "It was a very difficult time for me. Then I made the distinction—excuse that expression—between human beings and *civilized* human beings. I had to make that distinction. All small children were terrific, one. Two, most of them grew up to be appreciably less than terrific. What could a person think? Genes apart, only their civilization—their childrearing, schools, and popular and high cultures—could account for that amazing fact. So, being young, I fixed on a rough modus vivendi: people were fine, civilization wasn't. It wasn't much of a step, even though decades of work on the question intervened, to the conclusion that we're all born whole, that for centuries our institutions have diminished us, and that it's possible to stay whole, or to recover from diminution. That's what I have faith in."

10.

Transcendence

"Faith? That sounds suspiciously religious." Jerry feigned shock.

"You needn't worry, Jerry." The teacher laughed. "I mean 'confidence,' of course, which follows from evidence. Faith doesn't ask for evidence, on principle; it would be thought weak if it did. But perhaps we should talk about religion. We didn't last year. The Confucians had no use for it—neither for death nor religion. Since we began by taking up what Confucius let alone, and since religion has meant so much to all the rest of the world excepting China, let's take a look at it."

"Death and religion. It's hard to say that religion takes care of death if you've seen what I've seen," Eleanor said. "When people tell me that an infant's death is God's will, I feel like throwing up. I had the God's-will crisis forty years ago, when I got my first job in an emergency room. Music is my religion. Catherine can't get along without late Beethoven and neither can I. Plus Bach, Haydn, Mozart, and Brahms. They're the deepest solace to me, and mystery that doesn't patronize anyone."

"Religious traditions differ," William said. "Another tradition might suit you, Eleanor."

"I think the religions are more alike than different," Catherine said.

"Look, you can't sort all that out," Jerry said. "Different, similar . . .it's thousands of years of arguments and knots, if you ask me. Give me science, with our provisos. It has clarity and it has grandeur."

"Or, when it comes to that, philosophy," offered William, "if the world religions truly don't suit, and science seems cold."

The teacher seemed withdrawn during this exchange. When he spoke, it was with a deliberation that suggested a sizable challenge ahead. "We have no choice but to sort out the religious knots. Worse, we have to add scientific and philosophical knots. It's only then that we can come to grips with a project, a single one, not three, unknown to tens of thousands of years before cities, and a mania for the five thousand years of city life. Since for those tens of thousands of years, human beings were genetically identical to us now, something must have happened, and kept on happening."

"How can this project be a single one in the face of the obvious differences among religion, science, and philosophy, not to mention the differences among religions?" William asked. "For more than a hundred years the *opposition* of religion and science has been a major theme of Western discourse. And philosophy has had its own parallel and distinguished history. Surely three projects."

"I believe the three pursuits can be brought entirely under the notion of transcendence, William," the teacher said. "Civilization became obsessed with entities that couldn't be seen or touched, that were held to exist perfectly and eternally in some place beyond, a place that transcended, the everyday world and our senses. Transcendence infuses religion, science, and philosophy at their depths—or heights, I suppose, for devotees. It's the project of transcendence that I refer to as incredible." He paused for a moment. "I'll tell you what happened a week ago. I went into town . . ."

"Hard to imagine," Jerry mumbled.

The teacher heard. "I go in to deliver vegetables, Jerry, and for the coffee shops. I love the coffee shops."

"When I move here, to town I mean, we'll go to them together if you want to," Eleanor said.

"I can't wait."

The teacher picked up the thread. "I was talking to a teen-ager at the counter at Leon's. The boy was fidgety. He kept saying that he was bored. Nothing interested him. Do you hear: *no thing* interested him. Each thing in the world was empty of interest, of content, including himself. I thought, This boy thinks things, including people, barely exist. If they hardly exist anyway, it wouldn't take much, or be much, to tip them into literal non-existence, to destroy things, people. Not that this particular person would take that step, but the thought remained with me."

"I don't know if I ever told you this," Jerry said, "but several of my friends from the old neighborhood who didn't get away the way I did are in prison. I couldn't believe it. The first remark I ever heard about the meaning of life, in sixth or seventh grade, was from a kid staring down another kid and saying, 'We're born to die.' Being bored and violent was normal. Real nihilism was normal."

"I think that there are four temperaments," the teacher said, "but they're not the four we have from medieval times. The first is the nihilistic temperament—my teen-ager and Jerry's friends. It starts with boredom and can end in violence to others and to oneself. The second is the literal temperament. All four temperaments depend on how much weight a *thing* has, weight in interest, significance. A thing has zero weight in the nihilistic temperament. The weight of a thing in the literal temperament is so-to-speak, one. The thing is itself and nothing else. It doesn't mean nothing, zero; it just means itself, one thing. You'll remember that when we spent so much time on Aristotle some years ago, he begins his system of thought—our, the Western system—with that curious statement, 'A thing is itself and nothing else.'"

"That was one long headache," Catherine groaned.

"Of course!" Eleanor exclaimed. "Aristotle is the codifier of the distinction-making half of mind. He must have said that about a thing being itself and nothing else as often as he did because he's killing the other half of mind: distinction-dissolving means that a thing can be itself and other things too. One of the translators actually said that those repetitions of itself-and-nothing-else were more vehement than they needed to be. Sure. They were vehement because he was doing an immense thing. He must really have hated distinction-dissolving."

"He killed the third temperament, Eleanor," the teacher said, "which asserts that a thing need not be itself and nothing else, just as you say. It can be itself and other things. It wants this. I use Catherine's word: I call the temperament of distinction-dissolving the symbolic temperament. Egypt, not Greece. The Greek philosophers, like the Hebrew prophets, hated Egypt. The West was put together by those anti-Egyptian, anti-symbolic philosophers and prophets. We're all Aristotle's and Isaiah's children, and our world is the distinction-making world of the literal temperament. The symbolic temperament survives only in children."

"And it's the schools that reduce the symbolic temperament to the literal temperament," Catherine said angrily.

"Exactly. Systematically," the teacher said. "Many meanings for one thing reduced to one meaning per thing. The world of things loses meaning. In such a world, diminished people deprived of internal fullness and of full of things around them, want escape. Transcendence is the result."

"It's ironic," Jerry said. "One meaning is only one meaning away from no meaning. The literal temperament is that close to the nihilistic temperament. That may be why it's so easy to get bored in a frenetically problem-solving society. If you were in the symbolic temperament, buoyed up in many meanings, you'd be that much farther away from zero meaning and protected from the violence of nihilism."

"Also exactly," the teacher said. "And there's one temperament left, in its way a supreme irony. I was thinking about theory-making, the activity in general, in connection with the temperaments. If this theory starts with zero, goes to one, and then goes to many, theory-making itself seemed to require finishing with infinity. That is to say, there would be held to exist one thing with all meaning. And indeed that's what started to emerge in real life about thirty-five hundred years ago."

"Well within civilized history," William remarked.

"Oh yes. I see no evidence of it before civilization came about," the teacher said.

"If one thing has infinite meaning, what's left for other things?" Jerry asked.

"Nothing," the teacher replied emphatically.

"Well well," Jerry continued. "We have an unusual situation here. This fourth temperament—I presume the transcendent temperament—leaves all the rest of the world in the nihilistic temperament. All other things have zero meaning: simple arithmetic. That's troubling."

"Troubling indeed," the teacher agreed. "The nihilistic and transcendent temperaments are intimately connected, as you've noticed, Jerry. Unfortunately, that can mean that contemplation of infinity or an infinite entity or of eternal perfection can switch in an instant into such an under-valuation of some finite imperfect entity that relegation of that entity, or worse, occurs. Haven't you wondered how twelfth-century crusaders could so easily kill for God, when the Christian ethic condemned killing?"

"If a homeland is given infinite meaning, as it so often has been in the last three or four hundred years, an easy road to killing is again the consequence," William said.

"Zero is an abstraction," the teacher said. "You can't see or touch or hear it. Everything material has been abstracted from it. So is infinity an abstraction. I suspect the connection between transcendence and nihilism is there. Contemplating abstractions may do something to us. That boy in Leon's may find a cult to join one day soon, and he'll say something like he now has something bigger than himself to believe in. There he'll be, oscillating from one abstraction to the other. Who knows how dangerous he'll become?"

"At least literal people deal in material things most of the time," Catherine said.

"True," the teacher said. "But the nihilistic and transcendent temperaments were early made the constant handmaidens of the dominant literal temperament. A horror of nihilism can be effective in keeping ordinary people tied to the literal temperament, and the promise of transcendence has certainly been effective as solace for the death-terrors created by the literal temperament."

"The promise of transcendence?" from Catherine.

"Three kinds of promise," the teacher said.

"Not religion, science, and philosophy," Jerry said.

"Just so," the teacher said. "Religion, derived in the West and Middle East mainly from the Hebrew prophets around twenty-five hundred years ago, with a few codicils some centuries later; science and philosophy from the Greeks, also around twenty-five hundred years ago. Busy time."

"I thought you might have begun the Hebrew contribution much earlier, with Abraham or Moses," William said.

"No, William," the teacher said gently. "Those earlier stories are interesting, but not to the point. Transcendence comes with the prophets. They saw Hebrew armies being over-run by Assyrian and then Babylonian forces. The Middle Eastern precedent for defeat in battle was to adopt the war god of the victor, in hopes of better military fortunes. In order to prevent Israel from giving up Yahweh, the prophets argued that the enemy armies were under Yahweh's command, not some other god's. The Israelites were being punished for not living up to the complex demands of their contract with Yahweh. The severe punishment of erring children was a tenet of desert patriarchy; that Yahweh punished Israel was proof of his fatherly attention and concern. Conclusion: defeat wasn't defeat at all. There was now an explanation for suffering, even a heartening explanation. But everyone had to be put under Yahweh's aegis, not just the Hebrews, because anyone could be called up to punish the Hebrews. Conclusion: Yahweh had to be the single, universal God, not one god among others. It was then a simple development to an infinite, incomprehensible, eternal, all-knowing God worshipped by unquestioning and grateful children. This one entity was given infinite meaning; earthly things began to lose meaning. There have been few more consequential moments in the history of the world."

"And Christianity?" asked William.

"Five hundred years later," the teacher continued," the question of identifying with this infinite entity was raised to prominence. I refer to an actual boundary-dissolution between a human being and God. If you, a finite entity who will die, could remove the distinction between yourself and an infinite entity that is eternal, you could believe yourself to have defeated death. The question is the more pressing the worse your life is. Identification was difficult to accomplish, though: the infinite entity was far too different from you, and undoing that difference was just too hard. You could identify with another person, however; there the difference was manageable. So Christianity constructed a solution: one particular person would be proclaimed both a person, consequently identifiable with, and God. Conclusion: by becoming this person through ritual boundary-dissolutions, you would gain eternity. The religious promise of transcendence is defeat of death by this means. Oddly enough, the scientific and philosophical promise of transcendence is very nearly the same. What each does is posit its own infinite entity or realm."

"If there was one thing we learned about the Greeks," Jerry said, "it was that they were geniuses at imagining perfection and eternity. At the same time the prophets were claiming a perfect and eternal God that was inaccessible to the senses, Plato was claiming a perfect and eternal something-he-called-Being that was inaccessible to the senses. The Greeks couldn't stand it that what could be seen and touched always perished, since *they* could be seen and touched, and they would certainly perish. So they downplayed sight and touch with this Being of theirs. The beginning of the Western romance with pure thought, I guess. Do you think they wanted to identify with Being the same way the Christians, later, did with Jesus? Plato doesn't say so."

"I do think so," the teacher said. "The Greeks wanted the same thing Christians did, eternal life. The pathos of the philosophical enterprise from the Greeks on lay in their codifying the entire distinction-*making* program, as you observe of Aristotle, Eleanor, and wanting desperately to achieve a distinction-*dissolution* with Being. They couldn't have it both ways."

"Science isn't as abstract as philosophy," Jerry said. "Thales and Pythagoras invented science between them, and wanted perfection and eternity before Plato did. But they involved the senses. Well, not Pythagoras so much. He posits number as his equivalent of God and Being. Thales posits a material substance, though. That's a lot less abstract than the prophets and Plato."

"It is," the teacher said, "and that's why the scientific promise has borne more fruit in one sense. It has also produced less emotional sufficiency. And recently science has suffered an exaggerated quandary over the difference between reality and appearance."

"In Britain between the wars," William said, "intellectual circles were much occupied with what we called the table problem, our version of the reality and appearance quandary. A lecture by a prominent physicist opened by asking how real a table was. Was the truly real table an ensemble of incredibly tiny particles separated by vast spaces in which various forces acted? That was the table physics gave us. What we ate our breakfasts on was merely the apparent table. So did we spend our lives in a world of appearances? I was reminded even then of Plato. The eternal and perfect Platonic forms, accessible to heroically refined thought and never to the senses, were reality according to him. What we had from our senses was appearance. How the everyday world was lowered in our youthful estimation."

"The everyday world seems to get a battering from religion and then philosophy and then science: poor everyday world," Catherine said.

"When you take the project of transcendence in its three forms, and then remember its dangerous relationship to nihilism, and the support both transcendence and nihilism lend to the literal temperament of modernity, you see a tragic de-valuation of the everyday world," the teacher said. "What distinction-dissolution and the symbolic temperament do is restore the value of the everyday. Ordinary things are given their wonder back. Aren't pebbles a continuous wonder to two-year-olds? Nor do two-year-olds worry themselves sick about death. For an adult whose equilibrium is restored, pebbles are full again, time is full again, and death loses its terror."

"Transcendence seems to be an imperative of immature societies, then," William said. "It's odd, is it not? Religion and science and philosophy have been considered for centuries as among our most mature pursuits. We need to re-define maturity."

"The standard definition gave us the modern centuries," the teacher said. "More than a hundred million people died in wars and genocides in the last century. More than a hundred million. We have no choice but to re-define maturity."

"As kindness," Eleanor said.

11.

Art

"We've more-or-less done in religion, science, and philosophy," Catherine said. "I'm afraid we'll do the same to art. That upsets me."

"We've been completely approving of great music, Catherine," Jerry said sympathetically.

Eleanor added, "And surely art is involved with the senses, unlike religion, and with the gooey heavy matter you and I, not the physicists and the Platonists, know to be real. Art is completely different from religion, science, and philosophy."

"Why do I associate art with those others, though?" William wondered aloud. "In the Renaissance, art was part of the high culture that included the transcending pursuits—even its most resplendent part. It wasn't opposed to religion or science or philosophy."

"Art may straddle the fence," the teacher said. "I hate to risk inducing the Aristotle headache in connection with what you love, Catherine, but we can't escape him. Take painting and sculpture. When Aristotle spoke about art, he assumed distinctions among the artist, one, the subject, say a bowl of flowers, two, and the representation of the subject, the painting of the bowl of flowers, three. The artist imitated the subject with his representation. Simple. We think that's so obvious, at least for what we now call representational art, that we don't notice what Aristotle precludes."

"I've taken for granted the separateness of that flower painting, the flowers, and the painter, I admit," Catherine said. "It seems harmless to me. The question is how expressive the painter has been."

"There may be another issue," William said. "I had been thinking about art in the Renaissance when I should have been thinking about art before civilization. We've been making advances today by going back farther, just as in the French saying. Someone painting a picture of an animal twenty thousand years ago may have believed that the living animal was being created. There would have been no distinction in the painter's mind between the subject and the representation. Aristotle must have drawn that distinction in order to end the fusion of painting and living animal, in the same way his insistence on a thing being itself and nothing else ended the symbolic temperament."

"It goes on, William," the teacher said. "The artist could become the animal by putting on an animal mask. That boundary-dissolution, fusion as you call it, was the totemic doubling itself. Saying that the artist was a person only and the animal an animal only destroyed totemism. The apparently harmless separation of artist, artwork, and subject turns out to be momentous."

"One side of the fence is art involving the senses and matter. That's good. The other side is art participating in the destruction of totemism. That's bad. Right?" Jerry gestured accordingly.

"Somewhat schematic, but that's my fault, not yours," the teacher said. "Right, with complications. Renaissance and most later art, as much as it involves the senses and matter, also involves mathematical techniques like perspective, and a very elaborate canon of aesthetic judgment, producing one of the most highly valued hierarchies in civilized history. Mathematics and hierarchy are hallmarks of distinction-making and when intensely refined suggest serious disequilibrium between distinction-making and distinction-dissolving. It seems that good and bad are mixed on the good side of the fence, Jerry."

"What are we to do, then?" Catherine asked plaintively. "What about beauty?"

"Ah, beauty." The teacher sighed. "One of the ugliest of words. It should be struck from the language. I believe the aesthetic canons I referred to, establishing what is more and less beautiful, are largely concoctions of distinction-makers whose fields of operation are the senses and matter. Interest in beauty has done enormous harm, fixing our attention on surfaces when only depths should engage us. We know how much more attention so-called beautiful children and beautiful women receive. Their features have nothing whatsoever to do with their kindness, which is what's important. Civilizations are seduced by surfaces—excuse the alliteration. You ask what we're to do, Catherine. Make things all the time, all of us, out of wood, clay, stone, paint, anything that appeals to us, and judge no thing more beautiful than any other—just as we judge no person more important than any other. An egalitarianism of full things. And remember that becoming things precedes making things; it's the fundamental act of the distinction-dissolving half of mind. So now and then become what you make."

"Aristotle's distinction-making in art was most completely worked out for playwriting," Eleanor said. "What about literature? We're all avid novel-readers here. What of that? I'd have almost as hard a time giving up Dickens, Eliot—George, not the poet—and Dostoievsky, as Bach, Mozart, and Brahms."

"Me too," the teacher said. "It's a mixed situation, as Jerry might say. We live in a civilization, complicatedly deprived, and those wonderful books create concentrated and subtle imaginary lives. The books are true friends and teachers. We should only remember that a Scot who lived with a Southeast Asian kinship community remarked famously of them that they had no literature, but dreamt great epics every night and told them at breakfast. We cannot imagine twenty or thirty thousand years of that. Suddenly the few hundred great novels seem not less great, but too few."

"It seems that any high culture lost if equilibrium were returned to us would be compensated for many times over," William said.

12.

Memory

"The history of high culture is irrelevant, then?" Jerry asked.

"Largely, I think," the teacher replied.

"Then what are we to remember from the past?" from William.

"There seem to me to be times and places that reveal an unusual number of ways to be human," the teacher said. "The times just before and just after the origins of civilization are pre-eminent, of course. Taken together, I'd say half of human possibility is there; and some years of study wouldn't be wasted. For the other half, Confucian China, the Greeks and Hebrews, Newton's and Blake's England, certain people and texts. The point would be to scrutinize the widest variety of institutions. It's useless to read about ruler after ruler and war after war, as we've been instructed to do."

"I see the rationale for some of those times but not for others," Jerry said.

"Begin with origins—not fashionable in the profession right now," the teacher said. "On the far side of origins, we have the immense subject of kinship, for which we have little intuition. Kinship expressiveness, for example, was a single activity, music-song-dance-storytelling, as if it were one word. Then, on the near side of origins, division into separate, narrowed expressive activities, followed by a reduction in the numbers of people practicing each one, then their professionalization and hierarchizing. On the one side, subtle modes of preserving amity, with an emphasis on the elder-supervised marriage of the young, not to friends but to enemies. You don't attack your own grandchildren. On the other side, with the destruction of elder authority, the shattering of peace-preserving institutions. War on a new scale. On the one side, reciprocity as a feature of kinship; on the other, a separate economics, given over to calculation. The same for the boundary-dissolution preceding group decisions in the kinship world, becoming the separate, calculative politics of civilization. Equilibrium to disequilibrium. By learning what preceded our present institutions, and how they came about, we see the largest field of human activity. We then use what we know diagnostically."

"As in medicine?" Eleanor asked.

"Exactly. History is often practiced professionally either as an art or a science. That's already a problem. The artists attempt smooth and interesting narrative, as in novels, with the difference that their events and people are in the record. The scientists attempt the kinds of explanations you took notice of, Eleanor, predicting what they already know happened. Both the artists and the scientists tend to intone Thucydides's famous piety, that if we know history we won't repeat its mistakes. We forget that knowledge of this kind has never stopped anyone from doing harm. Clichés like that die hard. A few historians do try to identify with historical agents in order to understand them from the inside, but they're a small minority, and the artists and scientists think of them as a bit crazy."

"That sounds like the actors who practice the Stanislavsky method," Catherine said. "They become their characters."

"It certainly does sound like them," the teacher said. "Boundary-dissolution for the stage. The kind of historical memory I think might be helpful isn't like Stanislavsky, though—ironically, after all we've said about boundaries. I don't see the use of identifying with most of the historical characters we know about. Better to choose small children, a grandparent, animals and plants. The alternative to art, science, and

Stanislavsky is a medical one, as Eleanor observed. Learn what health is first. Learn what pathology means: large numbers of innocent people suffering grievously through no fault of their own is a good working definition. Study that suffering with a view to curing it, period."

"Period," Catherine repeated firmly.

"Confucius helps," William said.

"Enormously," the teacher said. "He reminds us that kinship can survive in a civilization. And he steers us away from transcendence. These two insights alone can inaugurate cure. We mustn't forget that Confucian China is no utopia in a book: hundreds of millions of people lived in kinship villages, unburdened by the projects of transcendence, for centuries. Some things were quite wrong, but what was right was magnificent."

"The Greeks and Hebrews give us the Western version of transcendence, right?" Jerry said.

"And the Greeks destroyed kinship in the Western way," the teacher said.

"There are different ways to destroy kinship?" Eleanor asked.

"Indeed," William said. "I've frequently thought Kleisthenes to have been the most brilliant politician in civilized history. Athens was a sprawling town before him, run by large patriarchal clans. They weren't the kind of clans we've been discussing, but the late-coming steppe clans that were as violent as the civilizations they habitually attacked. Still, it was a variety of kinship, and a complete civilization must break up kinship of whatever kind in order to create its impersonal, hierarchical bureaucracies. Kleisthenes came on the extraordinary idea of re-districting Athens in order to break the hold of the clans, and doing it in a way that persuaded the clans that their power had been untouched. The new districts were called demes, and the new social order was called democracy. *There* was an origin moment."

"My goodness," from Eleanor. "So democracy arises from the ruins of violent kinship—and *stays* violent—the way the first civilization, twenty-five hundred years earlier, arises from the ruins of peaceful kinship—and *becomes* violent."

"Well put, Eleanor," the teacher said.

"I assume you include Newton and Blake because of science," Jerry said to the teacher.

"Yes. Newton adds something to the Middle East, the Greeks, and the Hebrews. Rather, he intensifies a long-standing distinction-making prominence to the point of domination. We live in the three-hundred-plus-year-long Newtonian age. William Blake was his profoundest critic, around 1800. He correctly saw that Newton's single vision, as Blake called it, had replaced an ampler, fourfold vision, that what Newton postulated was a glamorous and terrible reduction of human consciousness. Blake called the reduction sleep. But Blake was effectively alone. His time wasn't a time of contemplation but of unreflective industrialization—which, like Newton's world-system, intensified long-existing distinction-making habits. Urbanization accelerated, some huge fortunes were made, new kinds of suffering proliferated. The planet moved toward becoming a single economic hierarchy of economic sub-hierarchies. That's what it will be soon, as we push our unreflective post-industrialization ahead. What a pity."

"Newton, and Blake's *times*, are part of the diagnosis, then," Eleanor said, "but Blake himself is part of the cure. Who else?"

"There's much to be learned from ancient Egypt," the teacher said. "Minoa, which may have begun as an Egyptian colony, imported authentic play into a civilization the way Confucian China imported kinship. And there are individual people. In France, Charles Fourier understood modern suffering as few Westerners have. He called his imagined, cured post-civilized society Harmony. You like that, don't you Eleanor?"

"Perfect," Eleanor said.

"In our country," the teacher continued, "Jefferson predicted that industrialization and industrial urbanization would militarize people without their realizing it, reduce them as human beings, and make them unfit for self-rule. He understood this at the same time Blake wrote of single vision. In India, in our century, Gandhi saw the result worldwide. He asked all Indians, including city-dwellers, to remain or become village-minded. They would then act moment-to-moment so as to restore India to its self-sufficient kinship villages. The fourteenth Dalai Lama's appeals to kindness and to happiness are encouraging, mature appeals. All the components of cure are with us, I think."

"Does this medical model apply to a person's life as well as to the history of humanity?" Eleanor asked. "Kindness and village-mindedness come down to individual people."

"Oh yes," the teacher said.

"What about individual memory," Jerry said. "Do we need to remember the origin of our own, personal civilizing? We were only babies."

"Psychoanalysis, do you mean?" William asked of Jerry.

"Something like that," Jerry said.

"Some people would surely benefit from the recovery of early childhood," the teacher said. "Some wouldn't, probably. That's a difficult matter. Remember William's psychoanalyst friend. If a person can't be kind or receive kindness, let's say, everything we can think of should be done to help him. There would likely have been something in his childhood—insufficient holding, not enough loving attention, perhaps violence. A kindly society ought to gather around such people, to provide what has been denied them or try to undo what was wrongly done to them."

"My father has so little memory," Catherine said. "He says he isn't himself anymore. A person is his memories, he says. It's terribly sad. And I don't think that's true. He's still my dad, memory or not."

"Of course he is," the teacher said. He took Catherine's hand. "Memory is absurdly over-rated. The most boring people I used to know had incredible memories. They told you the date and time of everything that happened to them, or they did the ruler-after-ruler historical harangue. Hero-worship, mostly. Your dad will always be your dad, and when you're him, it will be his whole self you'll be."

13.

Compromise

"I wonder if tiresome recitations of facts is related to the empty presentism we talked about," Eleanor said. "A way of stuffing the present with talk and making believe what's empty is full."

"Confucius distrusted people who talked a lot," Jerry said. "Especially such people with good memories as lawyers. Hell. What will I practice, silent law?"

"You'll be all right, Jerry," Catherine said. "You've got us."

"I'll hold to good ends, do you mean, even if my means are bad?" Jerry said. "Monitor me. The minute you say I've sold out, I quit and take up bricklaying."

"We're proud of you, Jerry," the teacher said. "You know that, I hope."

"Look at George," William said. "He's married to Catherine, the premier school-hater of our time, and he's a school-teacher. He hates school too, but loves children. He's in the school building to protect the children in it, often enough from the other teachers. You'll protect victims of injustice. To do that, you must know the law."

"Here's an analogy to warm a slum-kid's heart, Jerry," Eleanor joined in. "If you were going to fight the heavyweight champ, if you had no choice, wouldn't you study his moves, and get strong, and perfect your own boxing? You'd be a dead duck otherwise."

"That analogy works for civilization." The teacher laughed. "It's the heavyweight champion of champions. If you're going to survive it, you must know *its* moves, as Eleanor says. We decided that the proper position toward contests isn't to win, but to not play; and it's possible to step away from contesting with civilization. But it's very difficult. For most of us, some degree of compromise is best: step away when possible; learn the moves, so as not to be defeated, when necessary."

"Like putting our best efforts into fixing schools when doing away with them isn't possible, at least for the time," Catherine said. "Can we apply that principle to city life? I know that what's best is de-urbanization. But village-mindedness is a help for city-dwellers. There must be other helps. We live in a city: George would be heartbroken not to work in an inner-city school. He'd never abandon those kids. I confess that I appreciate being five minutes away from a first-class hospital, because of my mom and dad, and George's lungs."

"I felt committed to first-rate libraries in big cities," William added. "It's true that I now live in a pleasant countryside near a fine state-university library, but I can understand certain conditions compelling someone to city life."

"Oh my, it's hard for me to concede even a little on the city-life question," the teacher said, "but I've sided with compromise—we're not heroes, nor should we be—and the planet turned urban before any of us had a say in the matter. May I wriggle out of some of my embarrassment by suggesting that there are ways to stay human in cities—of course there are—but when, if, it becomes possible to leave, one leaves? I would hope for 'when' rather than 'if.'"

"Stipulated," Jerry said. "How do we live in the city?"

"First, I would go to the pound and rescue an old dog," the teacher said. "The dog would probably be killed otherwise, and you'll have an ancient obligation in a recent, that is to say, urban, setting: you must take care of a living being. The more trouble the better. At the same time, your dog is a superb partner in and teacher of boundary-dissolution. None better. You and the dog constitute a school of kindness together. With such help, and with your decision to be village-minded in the city, you have the foundation of personal equilibrium and social responsibility."

"That sounds easy," Jerry said. "Not heroic at all."

"Second," continued the teacher, "I would work out a vertical garden. There are resourceful people who plant vegetables in what look like soil-filled plastic cylinders with large holes in them and a bottom. About the size of kitchen trash cans. The vegetables grow out the side-holes, yielding food vertically instead of from the customary horizontal plane of a garden. These cylinders can be hung out a window. Growing some of your own food though city-bound is liberating; it's ancient in time and deep in the psyche, like caring for and sometimes doubling on your dog."

Catherine couldn't wait to speak. "I saw a vertical garden last summer. It was breathtaking. Walls of flowers and vegetables on very little land. I'd meant to write about it."

"The picture of apartment buildings with edible outside walls at harvest time is quite a charming one, I must say," William said.

"Animals and plants to the rescue," Eleanor said. "And music."

"In the cacophony of the city, music or madness," the teacher said. "I'm no partisan of electronics, but I regard having the Busch String Quartet, Joseph Szigeti, and Ernst Levy, all dead, here, on record, worth letting the turntable into the house. All the more necessary in the city. I would also embark on learning the violin, viola, cello, or piano—at whatever age. Playing as well as listening is rescuing, and equilibrating. Imagine sitting with three friends in your apartment in William's vegetable-garlanded building, playing a Mozart quartet."

"My own life in cities, even more as a lawyer among the winners than before, growing up among losers, falls into self-absorption in a second," Jerry said. "Village-mindedness definitely will help. What else would keep us from admiring ourselves, or bemoaning our wrinkles, in the mirror half the day?"

"Your dog," the teacher said. "I know what you mean. Nature can be brought in more. If you can, spend time on clear nights looking at the sky. Most of our distractions, and mirrors, are at eye-level. The stars have a fine way of reminding us of our size."

"It's odd that you mention that," Jerry said. "One of the things we used to do as kids was go up to the roof at night and look at the stars through a big cardboard tube my mom got from some store. As I think about it, it helped a lot. We got far away those nights."

"I think of literature as taking us away as well," William said.

"There's no lack of other activities to counter self-absorption," Catherine said. "There's nature, books, and there's the city itself, its sadnesses. You can read to the blind a night a week, or serve up at a soup kitchen."

"A grown-up rocking-horse in the bedroom?" said Eleanor. "Getting absorbed in your four-year-old self?"

"Absolutely," the teacher said.

"We forgot something," Jerry said. "We've been talking about evenings and weekends, vacations. What about a person's job?"

"A troubling matter," the teacher said. "Much work in the economy is meaningless, undignified. Cities are economic engines. Charlie Chaplin showed us in *Modern Times* how readily we become gears in the engine, or detritus spewed out by it."

"George found meaningful work, protecting children," Eleanor said. "And William taught all those years."

"Don't forget yourself, Eleanor," William said.

"And what you'll do in the future," the teacher said to Jerry.

"With your help," Jerry said, "all of you."

"Let's not ignore the quantity question," the teacher said. "Most people work too much. The city demands it. Then there are few hours left and little energy for rescuing and constitutive activities, and the city claims you definitively. It seems to me that here is a wonderful focus for our best problem-solving efforts—intense problem-solving for a short time to prevent falling into a life of problem-solving. Invent a home business. One, do no harm. Two, don't work past two in the afternoon. Rigorous criteria—a real job for our distinction-making talents. If the home business involves the mailbox, receiving mail and sending something back, then there's a route to eventually leaving the city. There are mailboxes everywhere, and much cheaper places than cities to live."

"Wait a minute," Jerry said. "If the law eats me up, I'll make grown-up rocking-horse kits near here and get a post-office box for orders. I'll lay bricks some other time."

"A contingency plan after my own heart," the teacher said.

14.

Dangers

"Sometimes I think we all need contingency plans," Catherine said. "I worry continuously about my children, everyone's children, growing up in so dangerous a world."

"In this regard, the old are fortunate," William said sympathetically.

"You learn the world's threats," Eleanor said. "Especially the disguised, insidious ones. You keep yourself and your loved ones as far away from them as possible; if you can, you try to neutralize a set of threats on some scale, small or large. Maybe you do that as your work, and otherwise you build happy days."

"The threats are many," the teacher said, "but they can be understood. Far too many people give up on understanding them, and resign themselves to accepting whatever comes along. Modern society reveals a clear, only middlingly complex anatomy of dangers. Realistic hope and daily energy result from the kindly, intelligent confrontation of this complexity."

"We know enough about language not to be taken in by virtuosity with syllogisms, right?" Jerry said. "The Confucians knew that, and refused to make a society of syllogistic laws like ours. They relied on continuously supported kindness as the principle of personal morality, and kinship, ritual, and an equilibrated education for social harmony. We know enough about Western education not to be taken in by curricula that develop half of mind at the expense of the other half, and not to be taken in by arguments for so-called socialization when kids need loving adults, at home, not other love-deprived kids in a competitive classroom. We can understand the real attractions of transcendence, and we can resist them when transcendence means self-deception, or the deception of others, or violence toward ourselves or others. We know enough about competitive power-relations in politics and economics, and their human costs. We know what to substitute for power relations. We'd rather have two thousand people sitting still in a concert hall listening to a virtuoso violinist—we'd rather have those people playing instruments clumsily but happily at home, and singing and making up stories, and spinning in waltz-time, than sitting, sitting, sitting. We know how much of the work in the economy is meaningless, and we have hopes for home businesses and more self-sufficiency and serious gardening than now. We know what an equilibrium of distinction-making and distinction-unmaking is; we know how to get it back; we trust people who have it back."

"Bravo, Jerry," William said. He paused for a moment. "Our time is unusual for its proliferation of dangerous objects. Terrible weapons, of course, but also less obviously threatening objects, believed in fact to be conveniences or diversions, and soon necessities. When Emerson worried that objects would mount to the saddle, as he put it, displacing human beings, he was prophetic."

"Like Blake and Jefferson earlier," the teacher said, "about the coming reign of Newton in the nineteenth and twentieth centuries."

"What objects are there, in the saddle, do you think, William?" Eleanor asked.

"Television sets surely," William began. "We can agree that television has contributed mightily to the stupidities, hysterias, and violence of the last half-century. I add the automobile. In a society in which kinship is as weak, and career-strivings are as strong, as our own, the automobile will guarantee the rootlessness and economic obsessions that excessive mobility has ever brought with it."

"I can't agree more completely," the teacher said. "Loving parents protect their children away from home and nurture them in the home: here we have cars literally killing children away from home and television metaphorically killing them in the home. William's two objects have accomplished something unprecedented. They've become parents, murderous parents! Human mothers and fathers have given their children away to murderous technological mothers and fathers. Childrearing can't but lay the foundation of a society, and our childrearing is a grotesque scandal."

"Television is phony nurture in the home," Catherine said, "and there are other screens, just as deceptive. The internet produces phony community the same way television-shows produce phony experience of the world."

"Perhaps we have a way to understand these technological dangers," the teacher said. "Catherine points to phony nurture and phony community absolutely correctly. Let's say that what we humans want, broadly speaking, is an authentic internal life that grows out of all, not merely some, of our faculties being in good health, and an authentic social life that looks like loving and authentic kinship. What the twentieth century gave us is an inauthentic, technologized internal life in television-watching, and an inauthentic, technologized social life in frantic automobiling and catatonic appeals to the internet. This baleful substitution is fueled by inauthenticity at the very deep level of distinction-dissolution: conscious attacks on this precious human faculty, by advertising agencies, in order to sell whatever their clients pay them to sell. Indeed the selling has everything to do with television, cars, and computers. What we see is a closed and terrible circle."

Eleanor shuddered. "I feel like biting and stinging creatures are crawling all over me. Shake them off; it's what we have to do, shake them off. That alone will make things better."

"It's true, Eleanor," Catherine said. "Just shaking all that off, not quote fixing television unquote or electrifying cars, but calling the century's mistakes mistakes, will go a long way toward our seeing things more clearly. Then some of the things we're concerned about will start to improve by themselves."

"If objects have as much force as Emerson and you, William, think," the teacher said, "there will certainly be improvement, and if we listen to you, Eleanor, Catherine, and Jerry, from our new-gained disengagement from these objects, we'll be on our way."

"Period," Catherine said.

Part II

The Texts

Two lists follow, the first of books, the second of recorded music.

The first list is made up entirely of novels. The novel has woven together the literal and symbolic temperaments more satisfactorily than any other literary form in the West. There are no books on the list in the transcendent temperament. The pieces of music on the second list come from about the same times and places as the novels. Their syntheses of the literal and symbolic temperaments, untrammeled by words, are the strongest the West has produced.

Generous laughter, like great music, is one of the sustaining human mysteries. It is the place to begin.

P.G. Wodehouse is one of the twentieth century's geniuses of generous laughter. Among his dozens of comic novels are

The Code of the Woosters and several others about Bertie Wooster and his gentleman's gentleman Jeeves, and

Joy in the Morning and several others about the residents of Blandings Castle

The innocence of such comedy is matched by that of several masterworks written for children and supremely rewarding for adults. Pre-eminent are

Alice's Adventures in Wonderland and

Through the Looking Glass by Lewis Carroll, perhaps the most brilliant of the simultaneously literal, symbolic, and funny books in English, and

The Sword in the Stone by T.H. White and

Charlotte's Web by E.B. White

The complete major fiction of three nineteenth-century English novelists should be read.

By Jane Austen:

Sense and Sensibility

Pride and Prejudice

Mansfield Park

Emma

Persuasion

Northanger Abbey

By Charles Dickens:

The Posthumous Papers of the Pickwick Club

Oliver Twist

Nicholas Nickleby

The Old Curiosity Shop

Barnaby Rudge

Martin Chuzzlewit

Dombey and Son

David Copperfield

Bleak House

Hard Times

Little Dorrit

A Tale of Two Cities

Great Expectations

Our Mutual Friend

By George Eliot:

Adam Bede

The Mill on the Floss

Silas Marner

Romola

Felix Holt, the Radical
Middlemarch
Daniel Deronda
In nineteenth-century Russia,
By Leo Tolstoy:
War and Peace
Anna Karenina
By Fyodor Dostoievsky:
Notes from the Underground
Crime and Punishment
The Idiot
The Possessed
The Brothers Karamazov
In the nineteenth-century United States,
By Herman Melville:
Moby-Dick
In earlier centuries,
By Francois Rabelais:
Gargantua and Pantagruel
By Miguel de Cervantes:
Don Quixote
By Laurence Sterne:
The Life and Opinions of Tristram Shandy, Gentleman
By Jonathan Swift:
Gulliver's Travels
In the present century,
By Marcel Proust:
Remembrance of Things Past
By James Joyce:
Ulysses
Finnegans Wake
By Virginia Woolf:
The Waves
By Thomas Mann:

Doctor Faustus

By Hermann Hesse:

The Glass-Bead Game

By J.D. Salinger:

Catcher in the Rye

By Saul Bellow:

Henderson the Rain King

Some of the pieces below are recommended in particular performances.

By J.S. Bach:

Six Sonatas and Partitas for Unaccompanied Violin, performed by Joseph Szigeti

Three Sonatas for Viola da Gamba and Harpsichord

Six Cello Suites, performed by Pablo Casals

Six Brandenburg Concerti, performed by the Busch Chamber Players

Two Concerti for Violin and Orchestra

Concerto for Two Violins and Orchestra

For keyboard,

Two-Part Inventions

French Suites

English Suites

Partitas

Well-Tempered Clavier

Goldberg Variations, all performed by Glenn Gould

The Art of Fugue

By Haydn:

String Quartets, Six of Op. 20

Six of Op. 33

Six of Op. 50

Three of Op. 54

Three of Op. 55

Six of Op. 64

Three of Op. 71

Three of Op. 74

Six of Op. 76

Two of Op. 77, all performed by the Schneider Quartet

Two Cello Concerti, performed by Christopher Coin and the Society for Ancient Music

Symphonies Nos. 100–104

By Mozart:

Sinfonia Concertante for Violin, Viola, and Orchestra

Two Duos for Violin and Viola

Divertimento for String Trio

String Quartets, K. 387, performed by the Janacek Quartet

K. 421

K. 428, performed by the Amadeus Quartet in its first reading, for Westminster

K. 458

K. 464

K. 465

K. 499

K. 575

K. 589

K. 590

String Quintets, performed by the Budapest Quartet and Walter Trampler

Quintet for Horn and Strings

Quintet for Clarinet and Strings

Quartet for Oboe and Strings

Two Quartets for Piano and Strings

Complete Sonatas for Violin and Piano, performed by Joseph Szigeti and Mieczyslaw Horszowski, George Szell

Clarinet Concerto

Violin Concerti Nos. 4, 5

Late Piano Concerti

Late Piano Sonatas

Symphonies Nos. 25, 29, 35, 39, 40, 41

By Beethoven:

Complete Sonatas for Violin and Piano, performed by Joseph Szigeti and Claudio Arrau

Sonata for Cello and Piano, Op. 69, performed by Christopher Coin and Patrick Cohen

Three String Trios

Complete Trios for Violin, Cello, and Piano

Complete String Quartets, the middle and late Quartets performed by the Busch Quartet

Complete Piano Sonatas, the late Sonatas performed by Ernst Levy

Violin Concerto

Five Piano Concerti

Nine Symphonies

By Brahms:

Three Sonatas for Violin and Piano, performed by Adolph Busch and Rudolph Serkin

Two Sonatas for Viola and Piano, performed by Paul Lukacs and Andras Schiff

Trio for Violin, Cello, and Piano, Op. 87, performed by Joseph Szigeti, Pablo Casals, and Myra Hess

Three String Quartets, performed by the Curtis Quartet

Quintet for Clarinet and Strings, performed by Reginald Kell and the Busch Quartet

Quintet for Piano and Strings, performed by Rudolph Serkin and the Busch Quartet

Sextet for Strings, Op. 18, performed by the augmented Vienna Konzerthaus Quartet

Violin Concerto

Concerto for Violin, Cello, and Orchestra

Two Piano Concerti

Four Symphonies, performed by Felix Weingartner and the London Symphony Orchestra

By Schubert:

"Wanderer" Fantasy

Complete String Quartets, performed by the Busch Quartet

String Quintet

Symphonies Nos. 5, 8, 9

By Schumann:

Four Symphonies

Piano Concerto

By Mendelssohn:

String Octet

"Italian," "Scotch" Symphonies

Violin Concerto

By Tchaikovsky:

"Swan Lake"

"Sleeping Beauty"

Four Orchestral Suites

Six Symphonies

Violin Concerto

Concerto No. 1 for Piano and Orchestra

By Debussy:

String Quartet, performed by the Budapest Quartet

"La Mer "

By Franck:

Symphony in d-Minor, performed by Paul Paray and the Detroit Symphony

By Chausson:

Symphony in B-flat, performed by Paul Paray and the Detroit Symphony

By Ravel:

Trio for Violin, Cello, and Piano

String Quartet, performed by the Budapest Quartet

"Daphnis and Chloë"

"La Valse"

By Prokofiev:

Sinfonia Concertante for Cello and Orchestra

"Romeo and Juliet"

Symphonies Nos. 1, 5, 7

By Shostakovitch:

Sonata for Viola and Piano

Sonata for Cello and Piano

String Quartets Nos. 1, 2, 3, 8

Quintet for Piano and Strings, performed by D. Shostakovitch and the Beethoven Quartet

Appendix

This is a schematic account of a somewhat broader view of what I have called "temperaments."

Let us look at six temperaments, two with variations. Each temperament will refer as before to the quantity of meaning inhering in things.

1. The nihilistic temperament

The unhappy remark,

"Nothing means anything," might be unfolded as,

"No thing means anything,"

"A thing means nothing,"

"A thing is 0."

"To mean" is given a naturalistic sense: a thing that means nothing does not capture and hold one's attention; there is no interest in it; it barely exists. It is nothing.

The speaker of "Nothing means anything" is a thing himself: he has no interest in himself; he has zero content. Not only do other persons, trees, and ideas barely exist for him; he barely exists for himself. Ending the material existence of a thing, not excluding the speaker, seems a modest act.

Each of the six orientations to the world of things produces characteristic utterances. The most innocent of the nihilistic temperament's utterances is, "I'm bored."

2. The literal temperament

The literal temperament belongs to Aristotle and to much of everyday modern life. Here,

"A thing means itself and nothing else,"

"A thing is 1."

A thing has one correct name; a word has one correct definition. The modern West believes this to be common sense.

The literal temperament likes to say, "I'm right."

3. The metaphoric temperament

Now,

"A thing means itself and something else,"

"A thing is 2."

The metaphoric temperament comes in three varieties, cold, hot authentic, and hot inauthentic.

Cold. This is the commonest kind, given to wit and irony. When a cold metaphorizer says (if I may use a shorthand),

"*x* is *x* and *y*," he means,

"*x* is *x* and *like-y*."

The metaphor,

"Becky Sharp is a fox," means,

"Becky Sharp is Becky Sharp and she is like a fox too."

This metaphor like most metaphors is a simile with the "like" left out. So cold metaphors are literal statements plus literary conceits.

Cold metaphorizers want to say, "I'm brilliant."

Hot authentic. This is the least common kind. It requires the recovery of near-atrophied faculties. In the hot authentic metaphor,

"Rhiannon is a swallow," the copula is meant: that is the heat. She is Rhiannon, a woman with skin and arms, and she is—not is like—a swallow with feathers and wings. Hot authentic metaphors assert the double substance of a thing, the fusion of two contents rather than a similarity between them.

Hot authentic metaphorizers are able to say, "I can be more than I am."

Hot inauthentic. The hot inauthentic metaphor also includes the meant copula and it also doubles the content of the thing. The hot authentic metaphor doubles for its own sake: it is a human good to be a person and a bird at will. The hot inauthentic metaphor doubles for the sake of a calculative end, like profit or power, chosen in the literal temperament. The reigning institutions of hot inauthentic metaphor are the advertising business and bad-faith politics.

In the one arena, the hot inauthentic metaphorizer says, "Buy this," in the other, "Do as I say."

4. The linguistic symbolic temperament

If we extend the predicates in the sentence—hence "linguistic"—describing hot authentic metaphor,

"*x* is—meant copula—*x* and *y*," to suggest as many more than two contents as we wish,

"*x* is—meant copula—*x* and *y* and *z* . . .," we arrive at the linguistic symbolic temperament.

I'm not sure whether there are three varieties of linguistic symbolism in historical fact. I can't think of a cold example. Of hot authentic symbols there are few, and they are the glories of high civilizations. The characteristic utterances of hot authentic metaphor are intensified in this remarkable orientation to things—to things that fill in substance as long as we wish them to fill.

The same intensification applies to hot inauthentic symbolism, perhaps the doom of high civilizations.

5. The transcendent temperament

It will now be clear that this scheme does not so much take up what a thing means or is, but how much it means or is:

"*x* is 0"

"*x* is 1" or "*x* is *x*"

"*x* is 2" or "*x* is *x* and *y*"

"*x* is many" or "*x* is *x* and *y* and *z* ..."

The scheme *qua* scheme requires,

"*x* is all" or "*x* is ∞," an orientation to the world of things such that one thing is everything.

Those committed to the transcendent temperament are not only likely to utter, "Hush, I'm transcending," but, suggestively, "Life is meaningless," since, if one thing means everything, no meaning inheres in the plethora of other things. We have heard something like, "Life is meaningless," before.

6. The pictorial symbolic temperament

The five preceding temperaments have all been expressible linguistically, in sentences. The hot authentic metaphoric and hot authentic symbolic temperaments constitute the fullness of things and of words by way of sentences. The pictorial symbolic temperament is always hot and authentic, and it constitutes the fullness of things and of words without the aid of sentences.

The medicine wheels of Native America and hinterland China are pictorial symbols. Their utterances are silent.

. . . .

Several relationships among the six temperaments suggest themselves. The predicates of the nihilistic and the transcendent temperaments, zero and infinity, are abstractions; those of the other three linguistic temperaments are concretes, in increasing numbers. Abstraction undoubtedly plays a role in the close relationship between nihilism and transcendence. Oscillation between the two may be seen in one manifestation in the mystical poetry of the world religions, and in another manifestation in total wars. Recall that not only world religions but science from Thales and the Pythagorians, and philosophy from Parmenides and Plato, are much in the transcendent orientation to things.

The literal temperament dominates Western modernity. The nihilistic, metaphoric—except the hot authentic metaphoric—and transcendent temperaments are its servants. Meaninglessness is the threat that pushes us back to literalness. That living in the literal temperament is exhausting calls for respites supplied by metaphoric activities. That living in the literal temperament is emptying calls for the solace of transcendent activities.

There is some hot authentic metaphor and hot authentic symbolism in Western modernity, but not much. They belong to other times. The question of the twenty-first century may be whether they can be recovered for our own times.

9 780738 830698